DISCORD TO SYMPHONY

A JOURNEY TOWARDS HARMONY

Dr. MYTHRI RAMACHANDRA

INDIA • SINGAPORE • MALAYSIA

ISBN 979-8-89415-958-4

Contents

Introduction

Vinay C R B.E.(Mech),
Dip.(Software Engg), M.A.(Sanskrit),

Vinay C R, popularly known as Vinay Shastry is a polyglot IT professional from Bengaluru. He has a bachelor's degree in Mechanical Engineering, Diploma in Software Engineering and Master's degree in Sanskrit and Linguistics. Along with his academics, he received a scholarly education in Sanskrit and Vedas from his father Late Sri C V Ramachandra Shastry. He was fascinated by the Vedic sciences and linguistics, which encouraged his studies in Kannada, English, Sanskrit, Japanese and Russian languages.

He started his career with a Japanese software company in Bengaluru, where he was trained in basic Japanese Language and was deputed to Japan as a Bilingual Engineer. While working in Japan, he continued his studies in Japanese language and secured international JLPT Level-1 certification, the highest level of certification for Japanese Language Proficiency. During his long stay in Japan, he has travelled across Japan to study about Japanese language, culture, Tantric Buddhism and their Indian roots. He has also worked with many Japanese University professors and Buddhist monks to publish various books, theses, dictionaries, Audio-Visual materials related with Sanskrit, Buddhist arts and Oriental studies.

His interests and studies in Vedic sciences, Sanskrit literature, occult sciences and Indology have earned him recognition in various fields. He has been awarded "Jyotisha Vibhushana" for his excellent skills in Vedic Astrology. He has been a key player in connecting various Indian and Japanese scholars, IT professionals and writers, with his multilingual skills in translation, interpretation, localization and training. He has been a Japanese Localization Consultant, Japanese language and etiquette trainer since two decades. At present, he heads the Dept. of Japanese Language in the National College - Jayanagar, teaching Japanese Language and Culture to the students of Data Science, IoT and Bio-Medical Electronics streams. His equal interests and skills in ancient sciences, linguistics and modern technologies have made him a student in constant pursuit of knowledge and learning.

Foreword

I was a little hesitant to write the foreword to this book at first. The hesitation was not because I know Dr. Mythri since my highschool days and I could end up applauding her work just by the virtue of acquaintance. But my concern was about the subject of the book, which seemed to be a feminist psychological thriller genre. My reluctance towards the same old fights within the family, in-laws and children, silent spouses, loud mouth mums and intruding 'maximum's held me back. And now, all of them are present in the book! But when my simple reading of her book turned into an interesting perusal, I decided to take up the challenge of writing something about her effort. Because, her work is not just one more stereotypic narrative. Her fingers, I could sense, danced on the key board from irregular black and white pattern to a perceivable sonata.

The centre stage of the story, the Iyengar Mansion is really a school of spiritual and psychological teachings and learnings! Mostly the elder roles teach and rest; the younger ones do the rest. And sometimes the elders learn from the younger too. But there are other times when intermittent roles start teaching, learning, expressing, sharing the feelings. All these happen with two pinches of 'love' - one that is needed for the life and the other, that pinches constantly!

The role of Avani, second daughter-in-law of the Iyengar family is almost the narrator of the story and hence the author's best projection. It is clear that the author loves and loves to be that role - Avani. So, from pancakes to pan-American trip, kitchen to Big-Ben, backyard to Scotland yard - all is there in the story, sometimes figuratively! Her style of narration makes you get a feeling that Avani is your neighborhood lady. The story somehow seems to have many expectable turning points but how it ends is what makes it interesting! There is so much of attachment of in-laws to Avani here, that the entire plot can be marked with her growth from Daughter-in-law to Doctor-in-law and finally to Author-in-law!

Fun apart, through Avani, the author successfully plays the harmonic notes in a mature way. Her attachments are worldly and wordy throughout the book, though she tries philosophically to show that there is no attachment - the moment you let it go! तत्र को मोहः कः शोकः कत्वमनुपश्यतः। "There is no attachment, nor any sorrow for a person who perceives the unity!" (Ishavasya Upanishad 1.1.7). Hence I rest my pen, leaving the rest of the reading for you!

– Vinay Shastry

23rd May 2024

Author's Note

Within this narrative lies an exploration of the intricate dynamics of a joint family, where love and concern intertwine with the complexities of individuality and belonging. Amidst the backdrop of familial unity, a silent war rages within the mind of a daughter-in-law Avani, a battle to find her place within the intricate groove of tradition and expectation. The characters you encounter within these pages are not mere vessels for plot progression; they are vessels of emotion, each carrying their burdens and aspirations. As the women of this family navigate the delicate dance of fitting into established roles while preserving their own identities, they confront internal and external challenges.

It is essential to recognize that the conflicts portrayed are not simply products of circumstance but reflections of the universal struggle to reconcile personal desires with familial obligations. The tension that arises is not born out of malice but rather out of a desire for self-expression and understanding. In depicting these struggles, my aim is not to sensationalize discord but to illuminate the resilience and compassion that emerge from the crucible of familial relationships. Even amidst the discord, there exists a profound love; a love that transcends differences and binds hearts together in the face of adversity.

As you journey alongside these characters, I invite you to reflect on the complexities of your own relationships and the delicate balance between individuality and unity. May the story serve as a reminder of the enduring power of love and the unbreakable bonds that tie us to one another. As you delve into the world within these pages, I want to clarify that any resemblance between the characters, situations, or events depicted in this book and real-life counterparts is entirely coincidental. The characters that dance across these pages are products of imagination, shaped by the whims of creativity and storytelling.

Thank you for venturing on this adventure with me, and may the pages ahead ignite your imagination and spark your curiosity.

Warm regards,

Dr. Mythri Ramachandra

Author's Acknowledgement

I would like to extend my sincere gratitude to the creators and contributors of the images utilized in this book, sourced from Google Images. While every effort has been made to ensure that proper permissions and attributions are obtained, I recognize that some images may be uncredited or fall under fair use. The visual contributions have enriched the storytelling experience and brought depth to the worlds depicted within this book. I am indebted to the vast community of creators whose works populate the digital landscape, providing a wealth of visual inspiration for writers and artists alike.

I am filled with gratitude as I pen these words, reflecting on the journey that has led to the creation of this book. From the early seeds of inspiration to the final flourish of the last chapter, my family and friends have stood by my side, cheering me on with boundless enthusiasm and genuine warmth. Their belief in my abilities and their relentless encouragement propelled me forward, even when the road seemed daunting and the destination uncertain. In their words of encouragement and steadfast presence, I found the courage to pursue this dream, to pour my heart and soul into the pages before you. Their belief in me was not only a source of strength but also a reminder of the power of friendship and the beauty of shared aspirations.

With heartfelt gratitude,

Dr. Mythri Ramachandra

1

Garbage, Cleared for Deepavali

Your mind is a warehouse of thoughts, but not all are treasures worth keeping. Clear out the clutter and make space for the gems."

– Anonymous

Deepavali is nearing and the air is filled with festive spirits. In a cosy street, a little away from the hustle and bustle of Bangalore city, was the house of "Parthasarathy Iyengar". An old home which spoke history of 5 decades, which had housed 4 generations. Vedavalli, wife of Parthasarathy Iyengar was an amazing and dedicated homemaker who was successfully running the home, of course even after the two daughters-in-law arrived. Vedavalli and Parthasarathy are staying with their two sons Sreedhar and Srini. Rather their sons and their family stay with Mr. and Mrs. Iyengar. Sreedhar is married to Sreeja and they have their twin children Rohan and Rahul. Younger son Srini is married to Avani and they have two sons Saaketh and Samrudh.

Parthasarathy Iyengar was a meticulous head of the family who refused to retire from the finance department of the house even after he retired from his work at the age of 60. The Sons were real gems, apples of the eye of Mr. and Mrs. Iyengar. The daughters-in-law were also very accommodating and easygoing they made the joint family a success. Since Mr. and Mrs. Iyengar were playing their second innings in house and finance management without giving a chance to the daughters-in-law, life at Iyengar's house was a bumpy ride and always the sons and daughters in law, their outlook and lack of wisdom were blamed. Though the sons and daughters-in-law had the best corporate smartness, they were in no match to Mr. and Mrs. Iyengar's clock and calendar-like precisions in management. The grandchildren filled the house with lots of positive spirit and joy. They were the pride of Mr. and Mrs. Iyengar. The biggest pride and achievement of the Iyengars was their huge ancestral home.

The out-house of the big house of Iyengars, which was meant for special guests, was rented to an old lady Seethamma who was leading a life of an ascetic and was on a spiritual path and was into study of scriptures. She was a personification of knowledge. The Iyengar family used to treat her with a lot of reverence and she was a go-to person for all advice and guidance. They used to offer food to her on special occasions as she never used to go to anyone's house. She had seen Mr. Iyengar since his college days, his marriage, his kids growing up, and getting married. She was like the eldest person in their family. Subtly she had conveyed the message to Mr. and Mrs. Iyengar that once the daughters-in-law arrive, it is their time to hand over the keys and retire from their responsibilities as per vanaprasthashrama, which is mentioned in scriptures and stop worrying about the house matters. But it was never received seriously. Mr. and Mrs. Iyengar had a strong belief that retiring is accepting defeat and displaying inefficiency in front of youngsters. They also had strong insecurity that they would be dominated by the next generation and they never wanted to be at their "mercy".

The previous day of Deepavali was a festival of filling waters *(called neeru tumbuva habba in Kannada)* for cooking and bathing, making it holy for pooja as per tradition. All the family members take oil massage, bathe with water with infused herbs, wear new dresses for Deepavali and worship the almighty and the source of light for life. At Iyengar's house, this was meticulously followed and tradition was passed on with a scientific basis rather than just a blind tradition. The senior couple had passed on lots of those tradition to youngsters which were very scientific. The month of Karthika, (winter) is the time when chillness seeps and Sun is not so fierce. This is the most conducive environment for a lot of harmful bacteria to thrive and cause infections. The tradition of lighting ghee lamps, lighting camphor and incense sticks, using herbal concoctions for taking baths, and using turmeric and neem for food and rituals will keep all the diseases at bay. There was a tradition of making Deepavali "lehyam" which was an age-old grandmom's time-tested recipe that was passed on to Vedavalli. The lehyam (like chyavanaprash) recipe comprised a broad spectrum of around thirty medicinal herbs out of which it was prepared. It was a panacea for all winter ailments like cold, cough, fever and stomach ailments.

This festival was special at Mr. Iyengar's house. But this time it was more special as two brothers of Mr. Iyengar and their families also had plans to come to Iyengars' place and celebrate it together. So, the prior preparation of sweets and savouries was intense. Lot of excitement in the air for the children. But the sons and daughters-in-law had hands full of work and Mr. and Mrs. Iyengar had a load of instructions. When there is a lot of work, it is amazing to have elderly guidance. But when guidance turns into an instruction manual, the younger generation finds it very hard to cope. They either develop an aversion to traditional practices or lose all their confidence and self-esteem during the process of coping. It is a very subtle line that can be easily missed. One's creativity is at its best when there is freedom that creates a lot of headspace and calmness. Though the daughters-in-law felt this, they failed to make the seniors understand this nor could they rebel. They were walking the middle path.

Finally, the day arrived when the two brothers and their families arrived from Chennai and Hyderabad to Bangalore to Iyengar's house. The children were excited to meet the cousins and they had made great plans to burst the crackers and have fun. The co-sisters had lots to discuss on the house front. The brothers felt very nostalgic and went back to their childhood memories. A tasty and nutritious food that was prepared by the daughters-in-law with great culinary skills under the non-stop instructions of Vedavalli. A tasty lunch was traditionally served on plantain leaves. Everyone relished the food wholeheartedly.

The next day was the water-filling festival. The previous night, some stinking smell started wafting the air around the house. Some felt it was the smell of a dead rat, some felt it was some stinking garbage. Since it was past sunset, they could not trace it. The next day early morning everyone woke up to the loud and angry tone of Mr. and Mrs. Iyengar. They were yelling at a municipal person who had not collected garbage for the past three days and that had spread all over the house making it stink and it was a huge mess. Mrs. Iyengar was very furious as she could not wash the front yard of the house to decorate it with kolam (rangoli). Since the guests were expected, the previous week, the daughters-in-law had got the house deep cleaned and had availed pest control services. As a result, post that treatment, the dead pests, rats and cockroaches were also discarded in garbage that was not cleared! Since it was a very old unrenovated building, which was no less than an archaeological monument, even 4 to 5 generations of pests also had made it their home! The stinking smell was unbearable. Finally, the sons and daughters-in-law ran from pillar to post and requested a municipality worker to clear the garbage by tipping him some money. This was a secret pact as Mr. Iyengar, an idealist felt that he was a sincere tax paper and it was the duty of the public service board to serve him without taking money. That too for garbage clearance. This could have been silently dealt without such hull and noise felt the daughters in law but they never wanted to utter it as they did not want part -2 of screaming in the house. Finally, the garbage was cleared and the festival was celebrated with full spirit at the house of Iyengars!

On the evening of Deepavali day, Vedavalli called her second daughter-in-law Avani and sent the home-cooked delicious, full coarse meal with a special rice and lentil paayasam (Sweet porridge)that was flooded with pure ghee jaggery and saffron with her younger daughter in law Avani to be given to Seethamma. Everyone was more than happy to meet Seethamma at any time of the day. They used to find reasons to go to her as she was a very positive lady with a very soothing and divine aura.

Seethamma was reading a book of Bhagavad-Gita in her spotlessly clean and simple outhouse. The ghee lamps were lit in front of the beautiful bronze idol of lord Krishna and the freshly strewn jasmine garland of the lord competed with the incense stick and camphor for expressing divine aroma. As soon as Avani arrived, Seethamma invited her with a welcoming smile. She told Avani with a smile, "I can sense the aroma of the paayasam that your mother-in-law has made. Please leave the food on the table. I will eat after I complete reading this chapter in Bhagavad-Gita. Come here and take this fruit as prasadam of my lord Krishna. I had offered him this morning. Come sit beside me. Rest for some time and go. I know it is non-stop work for you as it is a festival and guests are around." She gently took her palms around Avani's cheeks. That touch was a magical mother's touch for Avani. Seethamma continued her talk " You look so beautiful in this crimson-red saree. You are looking the same as I saw you the next day of your wedding. Keep this smile of yours on always. By the way what happened to the garbage issue that was on this morning? Is the garbage cleared now? Avani sighed and said "Garbage of three days had accumulated. It was so hard to tolerate!"

Seethamma smiled and said "Three days' garbage you could not withstand. Just think how much garbage we carry in our minds! For days, months and years! Have you ever thought? There are so many situations that are not so good or not so pleasant or favourable in our lives. We recreate them in our memories, give them life relive them and enjoy the uneasiness. Then slowly we play victim and develop self-pity. Because of this, we lose self-worth confidence and courage. Or at the end, we can also become impulsive angry monsters! It is a chain. The impact of mental garbage is toxic to our lives. Avani was taken aback by this profound statement of Seethamma. She was about to leave after taking her blessings. But sat in front of her to listen more. Seethamma continued "Now just tell me whatever situation or instance happened, whether good or bad, we humans tend to recreate it in our memory. We relive the emotion and feel good or bad. It is like carrying the garbage with us. Especially the uneasy ones. If we use our wisdom, process the emotion correctly, and tell our mind it is over and it need not register that emotion., detach the emotion and see it just as an event, we feel much better and healed. When we try to relive it and grieve, we start analyzing and judging people. we start holding others responsible and start the blame game, all these are like heavy burdens in our minds by which we cannot travel light. See things as situations, don't associate your emotions with them. Forgive, forget and move on. Don't you think by this there is more freedom and you travel light? This activity brings in a gift with it as "no expectations from anybody! We just should be smart to unlock the gift!" Avani found this so convincing. Seethamma said "I think whenever you feel upset Avani, start playing this mind game, bring that situation in your mind, visualize and remove all the emotions from it, the way you remove building blocks. Now see it just as an event and move on. It's a very nice mental fitness exercise. She said, "you take care of your mind, you take care of the world!" Avani was wondering about such a deep secret for happiness Seethamma could explain it so well and make it look like child's play! She was indeed truly spiritual and walked her talk. Avani experienced real Deepavali at this moment!

She silently walked back the passage to her home and she got onto the terrace. Seethamma's words had a deep impact on her. She wanted to stay away from crackers and noises. She was gazing at the star-studded night sky. She started reviewing all the garbage and dead rats in her mind that she was trying to keep alive. The way she was suffocated by helicopter parenting of her in-laws as soon as she came to this house after her marriage, the moments she had to hold back her excitements to share little things with her husband till the entire house slept, the inferior feeling she felt when her perfectionist mother in law proofread and re did all her work, The moments where her father in law used to get annoyed when she brought something to the house which was against his will, the moments where she could not stand for herself and had to abide by others' choices at home, the moments where she had to take care of her children as per in laws' instructions, so much of garbage since two decades almost! She realized what a burden she was carrying! She felt the dire need to travel light. She could not travel back in time to set them right. But she felt she could play the mind game taught by Seethamma. She could really bring every moment, dissociate the emotion and just see it as an instance, immediately focus on the present moment and feel happy and light! She closed her eyes and started. It felt amazingly nice to try this as garbage was getting cleared! She knew it would take time though.

I think we need to check the status of garbage accumulation daily in our minds by careful introspection and by keeping our egos at bay, just like we check the garbage bins at home. So much of the garbage we accumulate and will be holding on without discarding. It affects us and the people around us. So let us clean and nourish our minds wisely every day so we can eject each day's garbage without holding on!

Shall we start Deepawali cleaning?

2

The Excitement of Meeting Childhood Friend!

"People don't resist change.
They resist being changed!"

– *Peter Senge*

After the hustle and bustle of the morning, the sons, daughters-in-law, and grandchildren had left for the office and school, respectively. This was a truly relaxing time for the Iyengar couple, as they no longer had to worry about how the children managed the grandchildren. Although not "control freaks," they always guided the children on the "right way to do it." It was a Friday morning, and as part of the routine, Parthasarathy Iyengar had visited the temple. On his way back home, he purchased the freshest vegetables from a shop in the market where he had been buying veggies for more than three decades. The shopkeeper was well-versed with the vegetable timetable of the Iyengar home; it was that predictable.

Upon returning from the market, Vedavalli was waiting for him with a letter addressed to Mr. Iyengar. Mr. Iyengar entered the home, set the veggies aside, freshened up, and settled into his antique reclining chair. He took the letter from Vedavalli, opened it, and began reading. Vedavalli could see a gleam in his usually non-expressive eyes, surprising her with his excitement. In no time, she rushed to the kitchen to bring hot, strong-filter coffee for him. Like a curious kid, she awaited Iyengar to share the news.

He said, "Veda, this is a letter from Aanandu's son. He wants to surprise Aanandu on his 80th birthday by inviting us over. Remember, he attended our wedding and once was there when our Sridhara was born. Unfortunately, I lost touch with him as I got busy with my personal life. I couldn't even respond to his letters. I've often shared my childhood memories from Mysore Agrahaara with you.

We grew up like brothers, walking to school together, sharing meals, and exploring places together. He was like my twin. His parents used to send him to study with me since he was lagging in school. Not many people in his house had a Vedic background, so his mother sent him to our house in the evenings to learn to chant Sanskrit shlokas from Vishnu sahasranama and the Bhagavad Gita. She always wanted him to gain knowledge about our scriptures. Aanandu's son has invited both of us to Delhi to spend three to four days with his family. We should go." Vedavalli was also excited.

Both of them were quite excited about the trip, but they consistently shouldered the domestic responsibilities, even though it wasn't exactly their primary duty, and were deeply attached to home. Breaking free from this routine was a significant challenge. That evening, at the dinner table, Mr. and Mrs. Iyengar expressed their desire to attend Anandu's 80th birthday celebration. Their sons Sridhar and Sriniketh were delighted to send them, and daughters-in-law Sreeja and Avani were already envisioning an independent kitchen without Vedavalli's administration!

Vedavalli prepared her special sweets, including *athirasam* (a pancake-like sweet made out of rice), murukkus, and other savouries, and packed them especially for Anandu's family. The tradition of gifting homemade food to friends and family was a cherished culture and a signature of the Iyengar family. In an era dominated by chocolates and canned sweets glamorously presented in decorative containers with an expensive price tag, the homemade and thoughtfully packed sweets and savouries from the Iyengar family were truly exclusive.

The day of their departure to Delhi arrived, and Vedavalli was engrossed in continuously instructing her daughters-in-law on managing the home in her absence. Daughters-in-law Sreeja and Avani had no other option but to nod in agreement to the instructions given by their mother-in-law, who had proclaimed herself as an indispensable member of the kitchen. These instructions didn't stop in the kitchen; they extended guidance on mothering the kids. Vedavalli strongly felt that, as an experienced mother, it was both her right and duty to instruct her daughters-in-law on how to take care of the children.

Both her intent and the content were unbearable for the daughters-in-law, who used to feel suffocated and burn inside like dormant volcanoes. They could never speak their minds, as both Mr. and Mrs. Iyengars were quite dominating and had a personality type of "either my way or the wrong way." This big fat ego had been over-conditioned for decades and was challenging to change. By the way, they never felt it needed any modification. The bond in the family persisted only because the foundation was made of deep love and care for children. It was sometimes like toxic nectar!

Mr. and Mrs. Iyengar finally bid farewell to their children and grandchildren once the cab arrived to take them to the airport. This was a common scene at the Iyengar's house; even for short trips, their emotional expressions made it seem as if they were heading to the forest forever. Interestingly, this level of expressiveness was reserved solely for their house.

After these emotional farewells, the cab dropped the Iyengar couple at the airport, and the flight took off, landing in Delhi. Anandu's son, Ananth, personally came to the airport to pick up the Iyengar couple, which truly impressed Parthasarathy Iyengar. Spotting them at the arrival gates, he approached, sought their blessings, and introduced himself as Anandu's son. Expressing profound gratitude for accepting the invitation, he drove them to their home in Delhi, located in Defense Colony, one of the posh areas of the city. Anandu's son was the Director of Research in the Department of Science and Technology, Government of India. Mr. Iyengar was highly impressed to see that Anandu had raised such a successful and accomplished son. He reminisced about the humble life of Anandu's family back in Mysore Agrahaara.

At Mysore Agrahaara, Anandu had spent most of his time at Parthasarathy's house, alongside Parthasarathy's father and grandfather. This experience had a profoundly positive influence on him. The stories from the scriptures they used to narrate, the morals and values they elaborated, and the practices and discipline they instilled at home left a lasting impact. After matriculation, Anandu, along with his parents, left Mysore and moved to their village in Chennai. There, Anandu was fortunate to be mentored by his uncle, a biochemistry professor at CMC Vellore. Guided by him, Anandu excelled academically, securing a merit scholarship for his undergraduate studies and flying to Delhi's AIIMS for his PhD. During his research, Anandu found a friend and future wife, Sugama, who was his junior in PhD studies. After getting married, and with the birth of their son Ananth, Sugama opted for a part-time teaching career to balance both her professional and family life comfortably. Meanwhile, Anandu advanced in his career as a defence scientist, leading a comfortable life for the family in Delhi. Mr. and Mrs. Iyengar were delighted, lost in the story of Anandu's life narrated by Ananth as they arrived at Aanandu's house. It was a beautiful gated colony with a lush green pathway. The car stopped in front of a magnificent mansion, and the servants came to take the Iyengars' luggage. Ananth instructed them to place the luggage in the guest room.

Parthasarathy's eyes searched for his childhood pal, and there he was in a spacious veranda, sitting in a comfortable easy chair, engrossed in solving a crossword puzzle from the daily newspaper. Scratching his head for a word, he murmured about a eleven-letter word meaning absolute silence. A quick answer came from Parthasarathy, a crossword-solving genius: "Tranquility" Without even lifting his head, Anandu wrote the word, completing the crossword. With childlike amusement, he then lifted his head to see who had answered. He was dumbstruck—it was his childhood pal, his second self. He exclaimed, "Hey Partha! You! I can't believe this!"

Anandu and Parthasarathy went back in time, and their happiness knew no bounds when they saw each other. They jumped for joy, and Anandu screamed and called Sugama, "Sugama! See who is here!" Sugama came out eagerly and greeted Parthasarathy and Vedavalli by addressing their names. Anandu was taken aback. She said, "This is your 80th birthday surprise from your son. I searched and found their contact in your diary, and we arranged for this meet." Anandu was truly amazed at this secret pact.

While the happy reunion of old buddies was ongoing, Ananth interrupted, "Appa, you have a nice time with Partha uncle and Veda Aunty. I will go home, rest for a while, and come." Mr. Iyengar gave a weird look and asked, "Anandu, what does he mean by his house? He is not staying with you? Only you and your wife stay in this huge house?!" Anandu confirmed that Ananth stays in another villa two streets away, which sounded strange to Mr. and Mrs. Iyengar, who had always stayed with their children even after their children got married. Ananth bid farewell and left, while Anandu and Sugama took Mr. and Mrs. Iyengar inside their home. A cascade of doubts and questions had already formed in the conventional Iyengars' heads.

Knowing Parthasarathy's love for South Indian filter coffee, Sugama had exclusively arranged for a special blend and prepared coffee for them. Both couples began their chit-chat. Parthasarathy, curious, asked Anandu, "Why is Ananth staying in a separate house despite this house being so big and comfortable? This is such a posh area; don't you think it's a waste of resources having two houses?" Vedavalli gently asked Sugama, "So, you have two separate kitchens? Two houses?" Sugama smiled and confirmed it.

Meanwhile, Mr. Iyengar's cell phone rang. It was his elder daughter-in-law, Shreeja. Upon receiving the call, she asked, "Hello, Appa, the plumber has come to set right that leaking water pipe. Shall I ask him to do it?" Mr. Iyengar quickly replied, "No, no, no. You people will not know how to get it done. He will unduly charge more. You don't have an idea. Tell him to come next week and repair it after I come back home." He disconnected and instantly looked at Anandu for the continuation of the conversation from whereas they had stopped. Parthasarathy got back to his enquiry "Was theirs a love marriage? Did you not approve it? They didn't get adjusted to a joint family? Why? What's the matter? Despite staying in the same city, you are living separately?" Anandu saw his friend with a smile and could easily understand his pulse and his nature, which was reflected in the kind of questions that were raised.

Anandu smiled and said, "Partha, my son and myself choose to stay in separate houses. Good fences make good neighbours. That space gives a healthy meaning to relationships. We can have a clear vision and a better view when we look at things from a distance. If they are too close, the vision gets blurred.

I know that a few years ago, during the days of our fathers and grandfathers, the joint family system used to be successful. It was successful because the elders knew how to retire at the right time when their sons got married. They used to withdraw from all household responsibilities and seclude themselves for introspection rather than interacting and indulging with the outer world. They perfectly followed the protocols of what we call "vanaprasthashrama"(Phase of retirement)as mentioned in our scriptures. So, the Grihastashrama stage (phase of discharging duties towards family) was free for the younger generation to take over and lead a righteous life.

I always used to be amazed at the lifestyle of your grandfather. How he used to guide children and grandchildren by staying at a distance, and that too only when asked.

He has been my silent inspiration—no blame game, no display of victimhood, no complaints. He was always immersed in his reading books, his meditation, his disciplined religious routines, storytelling to grandchildren, and helping with simple household activities. He had handed over the complete responsibility of the house to your dad. It was an exemplary way of living. That is true detachment. Nowadays, lifestyle has changed. Youngsters are in a more stressful life. We can't expect them to take over completely, and at the same time, in their fast life, we retired people should not become a hurdle. I feel we should support each other, and at the same time, we should have our private space. So, both will have our freedom, and minds will be calm and clear."

These words from Anandu sounded like a blow to the basic belief system of Parthasarathy Iyengar. He had never thought of this perspective. Mr. Iyengar became defensive and said, "What do you mean by 'having space'? We elders love our children, don't we? Staying with them and guiding them will help in keep up our traditions and culture. Else, it will get lost. With the joint family system deteriorating, values and traditions are also deteriorating, Anandu. Don't you think so?"

Anandu replied, "Partha, I am in no way against a joint family system. If it is a good team with mutual understanding and letting go, it will be a blissful experience. Else, it will be hell. At least one person who keeps adjusting always will be truly unhappy. Home is where the heart is. It should not become an imposed punishment on either of the generations.

We live in our minds. It is the ego that rules most of the time. Very few will have the capacity to observe the dramas and stories that the mind plays and not dance to the tune of it. Such people will have an amazing capacity for introspection and taking the right steps. In earlier days, many elders who had this quality were capable of successfully managing a joint family. Those who had empathy and love and were ready to keep ego aside for the sake of happiness and harmony of the family. But as values deteriorate and people are busy boosting ego over knowledge, within the family, competition seeps in to prove who is right rather than contemplating what is right. Such families are disasters."

Anyway, let us not get too much into the debate. On a lighter note, our children, when they get married, only then we start seeing them as adults. Life opens up opportunities for them. They will be young energies with lots of dreams and curiosities. They will make mistakes and learn through them. We, as elders, should make room for them to lead their lives independently. When we keep instructing them, they will walk our lives, not their life. It is a parental tendency to keep helicoptering over the kids to ensure that they don't make mistakes. But their mistakes are like the stages of metamorphosis to become beautiful butterflies. All stages need not be perfect and beautiful. Sometimes the ugly stages are essential for a caterpillar to become a butterfly. So, let them be on their own. Being well-wishers, let us be in the audience and enjoy beautiful butterflies. Of course, they will come to us when they are confused. But if we hold their hands tightly and walk their path, they might be physically with us, but in their hearts, they would have cut the cords. That's a very sorry state.

They will have their dreams of keeping their home in a certain way, cooking their favourite dishes, calling friends over, trying trendy wardrobes, watching movies, and many more. But we cannot like everything they do, and when we impose restrictions, we are curtailing their growth. When they rebel, we play the blame game and feel victimized. Why? They intend to make their life comfortable, not to make their parents' lives miserable. Do you think our children will be happy seeing us in a victim posture? No. The best gift we can give them is to stay positive and happy. Not any real estate assets".

Immediately, Vedavalli innocently asked Sugama, "But a different kitchen... You are okay with that?" Sugama said, "I wanted my daughter-in-law to have her kitchen. I am a passionate cook. I love the art and science of cooking. I got an excellent opportunity in life to freely try my hands on the kitchen the way I liked; I could explore so many things with the aesthetics of my kitchen. So, I want my daughter-in-law also to have it. Sometimes, we cook different dishes and share them. Sometimes, when both of us don't want to cook, we will go and try some new food outside. Sometimes, when she has a lot of time, she will learn traditional recipes from me. Though she is younger than me, I have learnt a lot of smart tips about kitchen management from her". Vedavalli felt as if she was viewing some fictitious movie! She was thinking, how nicely Sugama is making her life so easy, apt to her name which means easy-going! There is such a free flow!

While they were talking, Anandu's daughter-in-law Gowri came in and wished all of them well. She said, "Hello Partha uncle and Veda Aunty, have heard a lot about you both from Appa. So nice all of you have met after a long time!" She said "today, all of you are coming to my place for lunch." She turned to Sugama and said, "Amma, it's a holiday for your kitchen today. You all spend time talking. I will prepare lunch for you all." Mr. and Mrs. Iyengar had a glimpse of a different lifestyle and perspective about life. A perspective that was way different from their belief system. So overall, it was a time well spent. They witnessed a happy family who stayed together in hearts despite staying under different roofs.

The next day, Ananth arranged a small dinner get-together for Anandu's 80th birthday, as Anandu requested that he didn't want any pomp and show parties. Mr. Iyengar felt extremely proud of his friend's simple living and high thinking. After spending a week with them, Mr. and Mrs. Iyengar travelled back to their sweet home in Bangalore. They were still recalling Anandu's perspective. As soon as they arrived, sons, daughters-in-law, and grandkids welcomed them back. Avani asked, "Hope you all had a good time in Delhi. Amma, what shall I make for lunch?" Veda replied, "Anything is okay for me, whatever is convenient, you make." Avani was in a state of shock. She pinched herself to check again if it was Vedavalli, a personification of fussy specifications, telling this!

Elder son Sridhara asked Mr. Iyengar, "Appa, that pipe work needs repair. It is an emergency. Shall I ask him to do it tomorrow? Since you are back, you can tell him." Mr. Iyengar answered, "You are the responsible man of the house. You decide and get it done the way you want. Why should I do everything?" Sridhara could not believe his ears. Avani and Sreeja silently murmured to each other. Like COVID-19, some other virus would have impacted them in Delhi! They both are just not themselves! Maybe once they rest well, they will take over the house at their regular pace.

The next morning, Mr. Iyengar was reading the newspaper on his easy chair and heard the honking of their regular plumber's old Bajaj scooter. He came out and said, "You people cannot handle this; I will get it repaired." Vedavalli came out to ensure that the plumber left his muddy slippers outside the house. She smelt something in the kitchen and screamed at Sreeja, "How many times should I say that? Don't use a high flame for garnishing the rasam; it will spoil the aroma of rasam. Wait, I will come and show you how to do it. Now Avani was relieved that her in-laws were perfectly normal! As usual, Mr. and Mrs. Iyengar resumed back to the thrones of their kingdom.

3
From Delusion to Delight

Just when the caterpillar thought the world was over, it became a butterfly!

– A proverb

Avani, the youngest daughter-in-law of the Iyengars and the wife of Sriniketh was a very soft-spoken and gentle woman. The way she integrated with the tough Iyengar couple in the family was proof of her resilience. Sriniketh and Avani had two sons, Saketh and Samrudh; one was in high school, and the other was in middle school. Avani worked in an NGO in the Environmental science department as a consulting scientist and had taken up a part-time job, as her preference was to give more time to her family and kids.

The love that Parthasarathy and Vedavalli had for their grandchildren was boundless. The care and affection they showered on the grandchildren were truly immense. However, in caregiving for the grandchildren, Vedavalli was ignorantly sidelining Avani, helicopter parenting her grandkids. This made it difficult for Avani to resume her role as a mother. On the surface, everything seemed perfect. But the inner turmoil was felt only by Avani that greatly reflected in their day-to-day routines. Vedavalli was engrossed in monitoring Avani's parenting, from winter clothing for the grandchildren to the snacks prepared at home and their hygiene. She took over everything as her primary duty. Mr. Parthasarathy Iyengar, also deeply attached to the family, took pride in grandparenting. However, the damage to Avani's psyche had started since the birth of her first child, which, over a decade, had become a slow poison, leading to negative surges and pushing Avani into depression.

The one who used to have a 1000-volt smile lost the light in her eyes. She seemed lost, experiencing intense palpitations and delving into insomnia. Avani could not resume her basic duties in the kitchen; she felt like running away from it. This became a serious concern for the family, especially for Sriniketh. Avani, once a passionate and amazing cook, withdrew from the kitchen, shocking others. She applied for sick leave at the office and started sulking in her room. She couldn't sit with her kids and help them study. The once bright presence of Avani was masked by a heavy grey cloud, and Sriniketh started worrying.

Despite sensing Avani's discomfort with his parents, Sriniketh failed to take any action due to his intense attachment to them. He was sandwiched between two important relationships that were not in sync with each other. One Sunday forenoon, Sriniketh's close friend Sriram and his wife Spoorti visited the Iyengar's house, bringing sweets for Vedavalli and chocolates for the kids. Sriniketh struggled to receive them warmly, knowing Avani was not in the right spirits. Spoorti noticed Avani's absence and, upon learning about her condition, suggested taking her to her aunt Vasantha, an experienced psychologist, instead of resorting to medications. Vasantha, a very accomplished psychologist lived in a farmhouse on the outskirts of Bangalore. Spoorti strongly felt that she could provide holistic support to address Avani's psychological problems.

She said "She is a holistic healer who treats many differently-abled children, depressed individuals, providing counselling amidst nature. The soil and plants of her farm act like medicines. Many stressed women seek her guidance, and she has empowered numerous rural women by employing them on her farm. The farm itself is a healing place. I insist that you bring Avani there; let her meet Vasantha aunty once.

I am sure the healing will begin". The suggestion sounded very promising to Srini. He agreed to take Avani to Dr. Vasantha's farm clinic in Kanakapura, on the outskirts of Bangalore. Sriniketh took leave from the office and informed Parthasarathy and Vedavalli to manage the kids in their absence. Vedavalli assured them that she would take care of the kids, expressing her thoughts on the challenges faced by today's sensitive women. Parthasarathy Iyengar continued emphasizing the support given by him and Vedavalli stating that in their days, the concept of depression didn't exist, Avani overheard this, and these words fueled her depression further.

Srini intervened, explaining that depression is not a taboo and is a result of setbacks in today's stressful lifestyle. He requested patience and understanding from his parents, alleviating the tension momentarily. He informed them about taking Avani to Dr. Vasantha for counselling, and after two days, once her counselling was over, they would return. Avani hugged the kids and struggled to be happy, feeling guilty for troubling everyone. Vedavalli reassured her, expressing faith and promising a trip to Tirupati once Avani recovered. Parthasarathy Iyengar also blessed her, and Sriniketh drove Avani towards Kanakapura. Despite playing their favourite songs, the cloud of depression lingered, and it became increasingly challenging for Srini to manage Avani.

Upon reaching Dr. Vasantha's farm after a scenic drive, Avani felt a breath of fresh air and dozed off to sleep. Srini was lost in thoughts about Avani's recovery. They were welcomed by the lush green surroundings of the farm, with a beautiful garden and a serene courtyard house.

The atmosphere was uplifting. They were welcomed by a huge inlay work of Geetopadesha, Krishna preaching Gita to Arjuna. From inside came an old lady, draped in a Cotton saree, with her thin reading glasses and a file in her hand. Dr. Vasantha, the psychologist. Dr. Vasantha greeted them with a warm smile, addressing Avani with positivity. She said "Avani, nice name. It means Mother Earth, a symbol of resilience, nurturing, magnanimity and many more. Avani felt a spark of light and smiled for the first time in a month. Dr Vasantha's welcoming words and the peaceful ambience assured Srini that things would be fine soon. Vasantha said, "Spoorti called and informed me that both of you are coming. So, let me hear from you now. Tell me how I can assist you."

Initially, Avani did not open up. Srini began, "We have been married for 15 years, residing in a joint family with my brothers, parents, and us all staying together in the same house. My parents are conservative and caring, a blessing for us. My mother is a perfect homemaker, efficiently managing everything. Even at their age, they are very active. My father handles the household finances, ensuring our comfort. My mother takes care of us all, making life easy for her daughters-in-law. Unlike others, she doesn't socialize much and is dedicated to the home. Our busy schedules make it a blessing to stay with them."

Dr. Vasantha listened silently until this point. She then interrupted, saying, "I understand your parents are actively involved throughout the day. What does Avani do?" Avani, tearful, looked at her, and Srini continued, "She works part-time for an NGO and is back by the time the kids return from school."

Vasantha asked, "Why part-time? Why not a full-time job? She is highly qualified." Srini replied, "It is entirely her choice. I've given her complete freedom to do what she likes." Vasantha gave a sarcastic smile, stating, "Everyone is born free. Freedom is not given by anyone to anyone!" Srini realized it was a wrong statement. Avani finally spoke up, "I take care of my kids, and my mother-in-law checks if I do it correctly."

Vasantha reassured, "There is nothing to feel embarrassed about, Srini. I am her doctor now. I need to diagnose the problem correctly to treat the cause." Avani, uncomfortable, moved towards a window overlooking the farm, where Vasantha suggested she take a stroll. Srini stood up, but Vasantha insisted he stay for a conversation.

Vasantha smiled and said, "First, it will be your counselling session; later, it is Avani's." Srini smiled, seemingly ready for counselling. Vasantha, drawing on her experience, shared that there is nothing wrong with Avani. She has restrained herself from expressing herself for too long, affecting her inner peace. She emphasized the importance of personal space within a joint family.

Vasantha praised Srini for acknowledging his mother's efficiency but questioned if he had ever acknowledged Avani. She explained the duty of a husband to make his wife comfortable and criticized the overindulgent roles Srini's parents played in Avani's life. Vasantha urged Srini to recognize the need for Avani to resume her duties, emphasizing that every woman's field of transformation is her home. "Srini, When a girl gets married, Society gives her the identity of efficiency. It is a role upgrade where she is efficient in managing a home, creating a family, giving life to kids, and nurturing the family. It is a divine role and God has showered that blessing on females. But when a man gets married, why should he be still under the shadow of his parents? I am certainly not saying anything against the joint family. Even staying in a joint family, each person can rise to the roles. There will be multiple roles for each in different compartments. You can be a caring son, Loving husband and protective father. But when roles get mixed up, then it creates a problem.

Men will usually be the breadwinners and get the "responsible" tag automatically. These days women also mostly prefer financial independence and stability. When a daughter-in-law arrives, her main zone of operation, along with her workplace, her "karma Bhoomi" is her home, her kitchen, and her kids. How can she be a shadow or an assistant to her mother-in-law? That is incorrect. A mother-in-law who has lived her life should just guide her daughter-in-law when needed. She can't be an instruction manual and stress her out in the name of managing the house. It is not her turn to manage the home anymore. When elders don't allow the stage for the younger generation and become competitors for the next generation, it is not fair. It will just not end there. When the elders become over-vigilant towards youngsters and find faults, that is the perfect condition for depression to seep into young minds. They start sending the children on lifelong guilt trips in the name of going against elders or not being obedient to them. The evolution of roles must be very clear to people. Else joint family will be difficult.

When elder and younger generations stay under one roof, the daughter-in-law will lack clarity and the son will be bound to the emotional narratives of the parents.

Vasantha said, "It must have been a long drive for you. Please go to your room and rest. I will speak to Avani. As a psychologist, I must openly discuss this with you so that Avani's problem is addressed. Kindly don't take it personally, but it will truly help both of you if you act on it. Currently, you both are living lives that are scripted by your parents as per their narratives. It is high time you lived yours! I am not saying you should not stay with your parents or take care of them, but roles will change as time moves, and one must rise to those roles. Your kids are learning from you." Srini was overwhelmed and needed some time for himself to assimilate this as he had never seen things from this unbiased perspective. He left for the guest room. These words, though intense, were an eye-opener for Srini, shaking his belief system. Sometimes the best advice is hidden in the advice we don't want to hear!

Vasantha came out of the house and walked towards the rose garden where Avani was standing and admiring the roses. Avani smiled at Vasantha when she came near. Vasantha began, "Now, let me hear about Avani. Please talk about yourself." Avani hesitated, but Vasantha reassured her, explaining that just as physical ailments are treated with the right medicines, the mind, too, needs the correct thoughts to heal.

Avani had thought of depression as a taboo, but Vasantha didn't make her feel that way. Avani felt comfortable opening up to Vasantha, saying, "I have been married for 15 years. I am naturally a talkative person, and marrying Srini is the best thing that happened to me. My in-laws are nice, but sometimes, their standards and rigid rules are hard to handle. I've learned traditional cooking, but the kitchen feels restrictive. I can't even comfortably watch my favourite movies or talk to Srini without interruptions. I feel constantly under surveillance, like a CCTV camera is always on me. My father-in-law is meticulous, working like a clock, and it stresses me out. I feel stuck, like in the office, constantly assessed without personal growth. Lately, I've been feeling too stressed and want to run away from everything. I'm not interested in a job, and I lack the courage to say I don't like being at home. I want my own home, my kitchen. I'm feeling so depressed!" Avani started sobbing. Vasantha interrupted, "You are not getting depressed Avani. Your mind is feeling so as it is in delusion. The mind is fickle, and what you are feeling is okay. Write down your feelings to create distance from your problem. It is outside you when you put it on paper. What are you trying to do to feel better?" Avani said, "A yoga teacher next door said pranayama will help, so I am trying to do it, but I am unable to focus" Vasantha said, "As a doctor, can I now take the liberty to advise you? I can't be a very pleasant speaker, but since it is medicine, you must be ready to swallow even if it is bitter, as it needs to heal you." Avani, impressed by Vasantha's approach, said, "yes doctor, I need help. Please tell me what to do".

Vasantha said "First and foremost, nothing is wrong with you. Just get that you're not your mind. If you like something spell it out right and raise to your role. If you give the steering of your motherhood to your mother-in-law and then feel bad, it is not obedience. It is foolishness. Raise to the role and take back the steering. You can offer a seat to your mother-in-law. But she can't drive your role. She can be your GPS when you feel lost. But when you are clear about your destination, you don't need a GPS. It is a bad addiction and you will stop trusting your direction sense and look forward only to GPS. Today it is your mother-in-law, tomorrow, anyone can be your GPS and instruct you!

I understand that when you got married, you were still in the process of adjusting to the house. In the process, a lot of things might have been suppressed and ignored. But you have walked this path. Stop procrastinating. First, learn to give yourself credit. You have taken care of your family and gelled so well. Acknowledge that. It's not easy for everyone to be inclusive and let go on a daily basis! Once in a while, everyone can do it. When the mind instructs you to expect a pattern of behaviour from your in-laws, husband, and others around you, and when it doesn't happen, you get disappointed. When every time it happens, it becomes a cascade of disappointments and there is rejection. So, you try to run away from such situations. But, are you solving your problem? Think logically. The answer is not to move away from the joint family if you are having issues. It is to change the approach of your mind towards the problem, rectify your responses, and take proper actions so you are at peace. Today you are not happy with your in-laws dominating, so you move to a nuclear family. Tomorrow you will face the same issue with someone else! But is your mind equipped to handle it well? The bottom line is, that switching on or switching off GPS for guidance should be your option and no one else's.

Agreed that your in-laws are parenting second innings. You are not liking it. But by not taking back the power, you are also signing up for it by not expressing your needs correctly. ***What you are not changing, you are choosing***! It is as simple as that. Check the stories of your mind and stop attaching emotions to them. Question every thought, and your actions get aligned. Write your script and command your mind to follow. Start being mindful and observe every small detail in the present. Say, see these roses, the petals, the shape, the green background, and feel the breeze on your face. Observe and start enjoying every bit of it. That is the greatest meditation. You need not close your eyes and sit with disturbing thoughts! Just get back with your loving self and take back the power".

This was like hitting a nail on the head, like a panacea for Avani's disturbed mind. Crisply, Vasantha had given her the message for Avani. She could feel the lift of the grey cloud from the sun. This was truly an eye-opener for Avani that she needs to work with herself so other things get aligned! After a long time, she could feel the sync and connect with herself. Tears of gratitude rolled in her eyes, and she thanked Vasantha by giving a gentle hug. She went to the room with a smile, and Srini was able to see her smile of Avani after a long time. It was a sigh of relief.

That afternoon, which shined bright for Avani, Srini and Avani had lunch with Vasantha's team. Avani could thoroughly relish farm-grown food. She discussed those recipes with the cook. They visited the women empowerment unit run by Vasantha Aunty. Avani was amazed to see the confidence and courage of those rural women who carried great dreams for the future. Avani felt that her problem was nothing when compared to the challenges of rural women.

At night, they had a campfire at the farm with singing, dancing, and sharing thoughts along with Dr. Vasantha and the team. It was a perfectly happy moment for Srini and Avani. The next day morning, Srini and Avani went hiking around the farm. It was truly refreshing. She could be mindful to observe every bit of nature around her, and it was so healing! She spoke so much! The happiness of Srini knew no bounds, to see his charming wife slowly bouncing back!

Dr Vasantha told Avani, "You need to come for the other three stay-back sessions over the next three weekends like these. The medicines that I would recommend are walking in bright SUN, deep breathing exercises, Frequent breaks from your daily routine, listen to your favourite music. Avani interrupted " Any restrictions on diet?" Vasantha immediately replied "Yes, some kinds of food are strictly prohibited. Not for the body, but for the mind." Avani said "I did not understand". Vasantha gave a smile and said, "Trying to please others, seeking validation, going on guilt trips, strictly not allowed!" Both Srini and Avani longed for the weekends. Life started sounding a little easier to Avani at home after that counselling session.

The next week, they drove to Vasantha's farm early in the morning. they took part in a yoga and meditation session. They had breakfast and got ready for a farm visit. They were amazed at the natural farm of Dr. Vasantha where they grew fresh greens, veggies, fruits, and lentils all free of chemicals and pesticides. They also visited the desi cows in the shed. It sounded like a different world to Avani. She was thinking about how happy those who are enriching the soil. Their soul naturally gets enriched.

She gave a warm hug to Dr. Vasantha. She felt as if Dr. Vasantha was a God-sent angel who guided her at the right time when she needed it the most. They started towards home. Srini smiled at Avani and held her hand with gratitude. He said, 'I have taken you for granted many times without even noticing your suffocations. I am sorry about it. Maybe I was blind not to notice. I will ensure that you will have your space at home. Now I am feeling that in the process of being a good Son under my parents' umbrella, I have ignored our core life protocols. I failed to understand your discomforts and instead, I forced you to adjust to their frame. It will not happen from now on. Let us start planning our lives together now. I needed the counselling more than you, Avani. Let us shift our room upstairs. Let us start having our physical and mind space. I think you can plan to keep the place the way you like. It must be your choice, Avani." Avani smiled with a look of gratitude.

Successively, three such counselling sessions were over from Vasantha's aunty. At the end of the third week's farm visit, Avani got inspired to revive her home garden, which was missing since she became a grey cloud. By the time they completed their farm visit, the workers had packed few fresh greens and veggies for Avani and Srini to take. Dr Vasantha had kept a few lovely lily plants with lily blossoms as a gift to Avani. Avani was delighted at the very sight of those beautiful lilies. It was time for them to leave. Dr Vasantha said "it was very nice to have you both with us here for three weeks." Srini did not have words to thank Dr. Vasantha. He told Dr. Vasantha, "You are indeed mind's doctor. Thanks for curing Avani's depression" Immediately Vasantha said "she was in delusion and not depression" Please keep coming. Not for counselling, but to enjoy the place and do spend time with us. Avani and Srini felt very happy with their warm hosting. Srini opened the car door for Avani and then went and sat next to her on the driver's seat.

It was a quiet countryside drive, and Avani started, 'How can you drive so silently? I will switch on my favourite music.' Avani smiled and said, 'I know you are a very slow learner Mr. Tube light, now let us go home.' Srini drove the car with his delighted wife, leaving behind her veil of delusion, which dispersed like the dust of the countryside road."

4
The Hoarding Syndrome

"Clutter is nothing more than postponed decisions."

– Barbara Hemphill

The bread in your cupboard belongs to the hungry; the coat unused in your closet belongs to the one who needs it; the shoes rotting in your closet belong to the one who has no shoes; the money that you hoard belongs to the poor. Your home is living space, not storage space. Hoard food and it rots. This is a great thought-provoking quote that everyone agrees with. But in Iyengar mansion, cupboards hoarded, rather hosted so many treasures, which were probably a little younger to the almighty! Both Parthasarathy and Vedavalli, when they got married way back in 1965, started their new life from scratch, all by themselves, unlike their kids who started their families in an established antique kingdom.

Parthasarathy Iyengar was an extremely meticulous person and was very organized in life. He believed in self-service for most things rather than outsourcing small jobs to others. If a tap was leaking, or there was some issue with the electric stove, or some minor woodwork, he would prefer to fix them all by himself rather than outsourcing it to an electrician, plumber or carpenter. He had engineering brains. His educational background was a diploma in electrical engineering. He was quite good and inquisitive with those skills and also wanted to save as much money as possible from his meagre income. He had the complete tool kit which had all the necessary instruments for plumbing, electrical kit and carpentry kit. This was passed down to him by his ancestors! So, these were his antique treasures.

His father-in-law had gifted him an old teak cot which came along with them to all rented houses where he stayed during his transferable jobs and later it settled in his own house. The maintenance was top-class! He had huge antique bookshelves which his grandfather had bought in an auction at the administrative unit of Mysore palace. That wood knew the kings and queens of Mysore! Not only Mr. Iyengar, But Mrs. Iyengar too had many such antique accolades to her credit. The heavy gauge antique Godrej metal almirah was her pride. This was sent along with Vedavalli by her father to Mr. Iyengar's home when she married Mr. Iyengar. That cupboard hosted her wedding sarees, her silver vessels, antique kitchen vessels made of brass, and the tiny frocks that she had stitched for her boy babies! Her secret cash chest, Various delicate gift boxes kits and toys that her foreign returned relatives had gifted her in that era, her sewing materials, Recipe books, old sarees, pillow covers, bedsheets, and many more! She always used to keep it locked and was the sole operator of that treasure house!

All the walls had a divine grace. The photos of lord Tirupathi Venkateshwara and Padmavathi, Ganesh, Krishna, Lakshmi, etc. Name a God, and the God was framed and hung in every hall and room of Iyengar mansion. The Pooja room was like choultry full of Gods! Not even an inch of space was wasted. Every square centimetre had a bronze idol of deities. The old teak shelves had various scriptural books. Some were just their enbloc which no one even opened and read. But since the holy book sentiment was there, they were lying in the pooja room. Vedavalli never allowed anyone to even alter the positioning of the items in the pooja room. Her God fear surpassed the faith!

Her Kitchen was an antique den. The lofts housed a variety of vessels. All heavy gauged steel and brass. Those vessels were her possessed proud treasure. She was obsessed with taking them out, washing them for a glistening shine and re-arranging them. Her recipes for all special occasions included those antique vessels too. Her pride and heritage continued even after her daughters-in-law arrived which made it very irking for the daughters-in-law. Her antique kitchen was a mismatch for their modern taste. It was a constant discomfort. But because of sons' strong and blind attachment towards their parents or complacency rather, no one had the guts to even introduce a change in the system or to move out of the system.

Getting his sons to study engineering and seeing them in elite jobs was the goal of his life. His entire life was dedicated to that. He dreamt a great life for his sons and it was so intense that he also started living their lives. After the sons started having their families, when they tried to de-clutter the house, all their old engineering reference books, some old tables and chairs, not even one thing went out. Mr. Iyengar was so scared that the sons would dispose of them all. So, he made room for all those things in a small walkway off the living room. But the clutter was amazingly well organized! Both sons, daughters-in-law and even grandchildren tried their best to declutter, but they could not even touch a strand of any of the clutter. Such strong was the bond of Mr. And Mrs. Iyengar for hoarding this old stuff.

Iyengars' daughters-in-law Sreeja and Avani were tired of the clutter at home. Avani was telling Sreeja, "We are unable to get any fresh energy at home. This excessive hoarding and clutter at home can have a severe impact on our psychology. This leads to feelings of anxiety, depression, and helplessness. The constant visual and physical chaos is overwhelming my mind, making it challenging to concentrate and maintain a sense of calm. This kind of hoarding by Appa and Amma, I think often reflects deeper emotional issues, and seeking professional help may be beneficial for both".

Sreeja, unlike Avani, was more tough emotionally and never bothered too much about this. She said the counsellor would go crazy if they seeked professional help. "Till our husbands take strong stands and keep their affection and respect towards their parents and practicality and convenience in different compartments, it is impossible to solve this. Why are you letting this damage your inner peace? If you can change this, do change, else ignore and keep walking".

Avani was very passionate towards artistically keeping home. She always felt that the Iyengars' great hoarding was a huge boulder in her path. She wanted to always bring in trendy dinner sets for the kitchen, modern furniture, nice study table for kids, but everything at home was extremely sturdy and carried an antique tag. Even Sreedhar and Sriniketh were fed up with this issue. They decided to declutter the house on a weekend in the absence of the Iyengars. In the coming week, on Sunday, Mr. And Mrs. Iyengar were planning to visit a housewarming ceremony of their friend. So, the sons and daughters-in-law decided to call 'Ratnavelu' on that Sunday.

Ratnavelu was the sincerest waste collector who used to collect wastes like old newspapers, plastic covers, milk covers, electronic wastes and miscellaneous from the Iyengar mansion thrice a year. He was a second-generation service provider for the Iyengar house. His father used to do it at times of Parthasarathy's father and grandfather. So, the Iyengars trusted only his service. Very little used to go out as clutter as the rest used to be well organized and kept.

That Sunday morning, the Iyengars got ready for Gruhapravesham. Vedavalli was looking beautiful in her crimson-red Mysore silk saree with shining diamond earrings and a nose pin. The strand of jasmine she had strewn around her hair knot was adding more charm. She was Parthasarathy's pride and daughters-in-law's envy! For various reasons.

The sons and daughters-in-law were just waiting for them to leave. They sent the children out to play as they were highly trustworthy spies of grandparents! As soon as they left, the hoarded treasure opened and Ratnavelu arrived on his old HERO cycle with his weighing scale to weigh the waste. As soon as he arrived, he saw both sons and daughters-in-law bringing piles of waste one after the other from inside the house hurriedly. They wanted to complete the mission before the years returned. Ratnavelu was still seeking something. He asked in tamil, "amma yenge?" (meaning, where is Amma?) They said, they had gone out and they also requested him not to tell them what they were disposing of their parents. Ratnavelu got scared! He was already foreseeing the consequences. He was even scared to collect that clutter in Vedavalli's absence. That was the level of hold Vedavalli had!

They disposed of huge amounts of plastics, old paper bills, old engineering books, broken vessels, etc. In the process, old pickle jars that were unused in the storeroom caught the attention of Sreeja. She took all four of them and handed them over to Ratnavelu. Finally, Ratnavelu weighed the waste materials and gave some amount to them. The sense of victory of the sons and daughters-in-law knew no bounds.

That afternoon, after Ratnavelu's waste collection rounds on the streets, he was riding his bicycle with huge gunny bags carrying all the waste back home. He had kept those pickle jars of Vedavalli at the top of the gunny bag. Vedavalli and Parthasarathy got out of the cab which stopped near the corner of their house street. After the housewarming, one of their friend couples dropped them back near the house. As soon as they started walking back, Vedavalli spotted Ratnavelu and called him. Ratnavelu got scared. He was paid extra by her sons not to come to their parents' vicinity. When Vedavalli called, Ratnavelu was about to change the direction of his cycle. She again called" Why are you going that side, I am here, calling!". Now, it was a checkmate for him. He went near her. She said this month he had to come home for garbage collection. Her eyes fell on those jars! "Ratnavelu, where did you get these from?" He started stammering and she asked him to take out those pickle jars. Ratnavelu felt as if he was a thief and he got caught red-handed! He cursed the Iyengars' sons for handing him over these old pickle jars of Vedavalli. Vedavalli could immediately sense that her treasure was being handled by her daughter-in-law. She got very angry. She gave some money to Ratnavelu and took them back. She took one foldable bag from her handbag and hid these jars. She didn't want an ambush with her sons as soon as she entered. The Iyengars entered the house and Vedavalli quickly rushed to the store room to place back the jars before anyone could spot her.

The sons and daughters-in-law were resting that Sunday noon. Evening for coffee they all gathered. Avani went to the store room to take the coffee powder from stock and couldn't believe her eyes! The jars had returned to their position, just the way they were earlier! She didn't react but gulped the puzzled situation in her throat. She made coffee for all and conveyed the matter to Sreedhar, Srini and Sreeja. They were sure that the war would begin.

Instead of raising her voice in her usual way, at the coffee table, Vedavalli broke down in tears. She said how sentimental was she towards those jars which were given to her by her grandmother at her wedding. She started, "You youngsters just don't value elders' feelings. We are not craving for riches. But we are attached to small things and even that is a burden for you all? When I see these jars, I feel the touch of my granny and her amazing pickle recipes. This generation of women doesn't even understand the value. In my house, in my absence, you handle my things." Till then Mr. Iyengar was indulged in his newspaper and coffee. The moment he saw tears of Vedavalli, he became very furiously defensive. He said "Even we are old. One fine day, you will throw us also out like these pickle jars. We have struggled a lot in this life and we have ensured that our children should be happy. But in turn, what are we getting back?" he went on and on and all felt very guilty and regretted they shouldn't have ventured into this except Sreeja.

Sreeja just shouted for the first time shocking others. " Appa and Amma, can you both stop it, please? Just because we decluttered your old things that doesn't mean we don't like you or respect you. All of us will have a say in a family and certainly, our views will be different. I understand you are sentimental towards certain things. But there should be a limit. It can't be so invasive that your children will not even have space for their things and views. Being elders when you have so much craze and attachment towards things, won't we also have ours? Have you anytime asked us what would you like? How would you like to keep the house?

Never! All the time you are bragging and stressing that it is your house. Your sons are so bound to you. You must be so happy for it. But, have you ever realized that your kingdom of antiques and hoarded waste is so suffocating for your daughters-in-law?" This statement was a real shock for everyone around. No one could even swallow it!

Sreeja continued "No doubt about the fact that we are ever grateful for making our lives so comfortable providing us all the help. But, please allow us to feel it is our home too. We have our tastes and requirements which will not match yours. When two generations are staying in a joint family, I understand that there will be compromises. But being elders, when you become so rigid, where is the platform for the younger generation to live life the way we want? The kind of young generation who are like extremists sound more relevant sometimes. They just cut the cords, go and live their life on their terms. We have some ethics and values because of which we adjust to elders. But you people will not even acknowledge that. So much hoarded clutter! my God! Sounds as if this is just a storehouse and not a residing house. What we don't use for six months, we will not use it forever. Then why have we hoarded so much stuff? It creates toxic energy at home. When there is clutter, the mind will not breathe. Please try to understand.

Won't we feel like inviting home our friends, furnishing the house in new ways, have new dreams? It is so embarrassing to even call anyone home with so much clutter. Feels as if there is no space! this is the reason we meet our friends outside the home at restaurants. When we can't feel at home at our own house where else we can feel so? Your children and daughters-in-law are not your possessions. They also have their life and their dreams and you cannot live our lives!" The more she spoke, the more anger got churned out. She choked and broke to tears with fuming anger and for the first time, everyone witnessed the strong yet cool Sreeja break down! The Iyengar couple could not digest it. Parthasarathy Iyengar turned towards his sons and said "I haven't forced anyone of you to stay with me. If my house and my ways are hindrances to you, then you can walk out and have your lives. I am not dependent on anyone. You please go out and have your free lifestyle".

Avani felt very disturbed with his reaction, his big fat ego refused to budge. She could make out that the children need to adjust here and no way the elders would budge. Compromise was one way traffic from side of younger generation at Iyengar mansion. All of them dispersed from the coffee table with not so good feeling. Sreeja and Avani went out for a walk and the sons cluelessly went to the terrace to assimilate the scene that happened. The kids returned after a day-long play and resumed back to their rooms they could sense that the pulse of the home was not normal.

The next day morning, Avani came to the store room and noticed that the pickle jars were missing. Vedavalli came and told her with a smiling face, "I want my daughters-in-law to be happy and not to feel sad so I have sent it to my sister Saroja's house. Today morning, Srini's friend Jayaram came. He told me that he was going to Chennai. So, I packed it safely in a bag and sent it with him. I gave him her address and he promised he would deliver the jars to her". Avani was shocked! "Amma he is going on an official visit and with him you sent those old jars?" She said "he is Srini's childhood friend. He will not mistakes. At least even I will be happy that the jars are with my sister and not with others". Avani was dumb stuck!

Sreedhar was getting ready for to office on Monday morning and found that the huge cupboard which was like an obstacle in the walking path was missing! Mr. Iyengar was sitting on his easy chair and reading a newspaper. He said, "Today morning while walking in the park I met Sreeja's parents. They said they wanted to buy an almirah and since they felt I have a good knowledge about furniture, they wanted my suggestion as to what to buy. I told them not to unnecessarily spend on that. I told them that I had one extra antique cupboard and I sent it to their house". Sreeja heard this and almost fainted. The cupboard which used to trigger her anger, now whenever she had to visit her parents' house, two roads away, she had to see it there!

The hoarded things at Iyengars' mansion were like real ENERGY. It could neither be created nor destroyed. But it could change its form and place!

5
The Guilt Trip

"The moment a woman decides to release herself from the chains of guilt is the moment she truly begins to live."

– *Anonymous*

It was a Friday morning, and Avani arrived at her office to find a letter awaiting her on her desk. The sender was Dr. Arundhati Rao, an eminent environmentalist heading the Department of Ecology and Environment, Government of Karnataka. Dr Rao had extended an invitation to Avani to represent Karnataka state at their five-day international environment conference in London, considered one of the most prestigious and significant eco summits globally. Avani, employed at the NGO "Dharitri," dedicated to environmental causes, was a valuable asset due to her powerful speaking skills. Those who observed her both at home and in the workplace sometimes wondered if she had a split personality. Her demeanour at home was accommodating, never refusing anything, while at the office, she embodied absolute clarity and professionalism.

She was chosen to speak about the threat to western ghats due to plastic pollution. Western Ghats, a green identity for a part of Karnataka, was facing a painful problem with contamination of plastics and disposables which was a toxic courtesy by the ignorant travellers. Also, because of lack of awareness, even the tribals who had petty shops around the forest for their livelihood started using plastics for packaging which was very hazardous to the environment. Karnataka Government's Dept. of Ecology and Environment had chosen Avani from the NGO Dharitri to present this topic on the international platform. Avani was excited about this opportunity and this great trip to her dream destination, London. Since her childhood, she was a connoisseur of art and literature and the poetries of William Wordsworth and the works of a few British authors had a deep impact on her. Her grandfather was a scholar and his influence on her was very deep. Since her childhood, it was her dream to visit London. But in her mind, the "Guilt trip" of moving away from house responsibilities had already seeped in!

That day, at the tea break at the office, Avani looked a little confused. She was thinking about how to take off from home for a week leaving kids behind. Her colleague and good friend Chetana, knowing Avani, started bursting out into laughter seeing Avani's worried face. They were soul friends and though each one never opened their mouth, the other could read the subtitles on the face! Chetana made fun of Avani saying "Talking on an international podium is a cakewalk for you Avani, but taking no objection certificate from your home team, especially in-laws is a herculean task for you" Avani felt that it was a checkmate by her friend to catch her emotion. Chetana said "Avani, it is high time you should be bold and take decisions for yourself. You have not signed up to serve everyone at home. Everyone is an adult. They are accountable for themselves. I know your role at home is crucial, but when you also have an official work outside, they will figure out alternatives. Don't make yourself an indispensable component. I do understand kids are dependent. But Srini is there to manage for a week, right? When he is out of the country for official work for weeks together you manage without saying a word! I don't even understand why you need to worry when your in-laws, like helicopters, are taking care of all of you. As soon as Chetana said this statement. Even Avani started laughing.

Sometimes, because of internally set moral standards, or absorbing a very strong and rigid sense of right or wrong, we nurture guilt in us. As the saying goes, "Guilt is rooted in actions of the past, perpetuated in lack of action in the present and delivered in future as pain and suffering." Guilt can either hold us back from growing or it can show us what we need to change in our life. Avani, a very deep and emotional person, in the process of doing her duties perfectly and rising to her roles, somewhere she was too hard on herself and whenever she had to refrain from her routine pattern of duties, she used to hoard guilt. This was telling on her inner peace. This was a very bad spiral for her. Though it is never significant to others, she was struggling to come out of this. Every day, battling with her own created guilt was a vicious loop. Sometimes we can climb mountains, but we stumble on pebbles!

Avani was back home in the evening. At the dinner table, she wanted to convey about the opportunity she had got. Travel was part and parcel of the people at Iyengar mansion. Both sons and elder daughter-in-law were in the corporate world. Avani was the only one who never tested the waters of corporate life. So, even a week of upcoming travel sounded big for her. Before even Avani could express it, Mr Iyengar expressed that he had plans to organize a south India trip for the entire family as the kids also had holidays for school for the Dasara festival. The last 4 days of Dasara happened to be a holiday for Sreeja, Sridhara and Srini too. So, all were excited. Avani almost choked out of guilt! She expressed that she has been chosen to go to London, and she will be one of the speakers at the conference. It made everyone take a second look towards Avani. It was more a shock than a surprise. Kids were super excited at hearing the news. Sreeja congratulated Avani for this nice opportunity. Even Sridhara and Srini were happy. Vedavalli's immediate statement was "But we have planned for the trip. Also, I have plans for the festival at home. Tell them you can't go this time" Mr. Iyengar immediately said "I was so much looking forward to a family trip. But something or the other comes up. All the other three will be taking turns to travel. This time so surprisingly even Avani has travel plans. Anyway, we will plan later". Avani said, "Please you all go. Don't cancel the trip for my sake. This is a very nice opportunity I have got and I need to go as my office is sending me. I Can't say no".

All dispersed as if their vacation got cancelled. Srini pepped her up saying, "Come on Avani, celebrate this opportunity. The south India trip we can go anytime". But Avani said "Appa was so eager to take us all on vacation. I am leaving behind kids also. That too when they have vacation. I am supposed to give time for family" Sreeni said, "It is ok. Now please stop worrying about it. Get ready to fly to London next week!"

Mr. and Mrs. Iyengar were very skeptical about Avani travelling alone to London. This was her first solo international trip. Though they were extremely confident of Avani managing household matters, (which they never had openly acknowledged) they were very sceptical about Avani's efficiency in the outside world as they had seen her over-domesticated! Vedavalli had already started packing home food for her travel. Mr. Iyengar was concerned about how she would manage her credit cards and foreign exchange! He was saying "Avani you need to be careful. If you see a beautiful flower or a tree, you will forget your luggage also. So please be alert" Avani was tired of these helicopter comments. In the long run, when others fail to treat you as an adult, you will lose love for others as well as yourself.

Avani found herself engrossed in introspective dialogue, lamenting, "I don't know when they will begin to trust my abilities. Even if I perform flawlessly, they manage to find fault somehow." The turmoil within her was insurmountable, and she struggled to convey it to anyone. During discussions with Srini, a recurring solution emerged: "Just ignore it." Occasionally, the discourse concluded with all blame pointing towards Avani. Consequently, every battle and explanation led her to the guilt station, where she reluctantly boarded the bus on a circuitous road of guilt. As these situations persisted, an indelible impression formed, leaving Avani deeply affected.

The next day, at the office, Avani went to the Director of her organization to figure out if someone else could represent her at the London Conference. He said "Avani, this is not some office work where we can figure out Plan B for the official. We have chosen you as you are capable of presenting the posters and topics very well. It is just a matter of a week. Please make sure that you go" Avani could not say a word more. She returned with a sad and confused mood. As she was coming out, she saw her friend Chetana standing right in front of her. She could get the pulse of Avani and she had already figured out why Avani went to the director's cabin.

She was wild on Avani. She dragged her to the cafeteria upstairs and blurted out at her. "Avani, please stop punishing yourself like this by feeling guilty for no reason. Guilt is a by-product of a lack of self-love. When you are not fair to yourself, you feel guilty for other's mistakes too. If your family is planning for a vacation, it is because it is feasible for them. For you, it is not. Say no without any emotions attached to it. If they are worried you are incapable of managing an international trip all by yourself, so be it, let them think. Why do you need to get affected or need to justify or explain them? First, stop seeking your family's validation for your identity, Period. Your love and affection towards them are different from your point of view about yourself. Please keep them separate. The more you try to adjust to everyone, every time, the more uncomfortable you will feel. I am telling you; this is a never-ending loop. Stop attaching your entire family for all the professional things you take up. This is your dream assignment and you have earned it. Why can't you say I want to go instead of "I have to go"? This will become a never-ending journey". Avani felt Chetana was showing her a mirror. She was always grateful for such a nice and truthful friend. She just gave a hug to Chetana and thanked her for guiding her in the right way. Chetana said "That is like my girl, London is waiting for you Avani, get ready and live every moment of your trip. Your world will be waiting for you at home till you come back. It will be safe. Don't worry!" So, Avani got ready for the upcoming conference.

Within a week, her visa got stamped and tickets arrived. She packed her thermal wear, some emergency home food, a thermal flask, medicines clothing etc. It was a different feeling for Avani. For the first time, she was packing stuff only for herself. All her travel packing used to start with food, clothing and medicines for children and in-laws and then the things she used to pack as a checklist and with last priority. Vedavalli asked Avani, what will you wear for the conference? Avani replied "My favourite Cotton saree" Vedavalli said," but none of them over there will wear sarees like us right? Won't you feel odd? "Avani said, "Amma, saree is the most comfortable costume for me and I feel it looks elegant so it should not matter". Vedavalli got a huge bag stuffed with all homemade ready-to-eat foods and munchies. The food bag was bigger than her suitcase! Srini started laughing. "Avani is not opening any Indian food shops in London. She is going to a conference. Let her travel light" .He also made fun of Avani. "I am not surprised if you feel guilty for not taking foods that Amma has made exclusively for you! You might take both suitcase and food bag!" Avani gave a stern look at Srini. She picked a few from the food bag and asked Vedavalli to use the rest at home.

It was Friday night, and the cab arrived. Srini, Sridhara and Sreeja accompanied Avani to see her off at the airport. On the way, they were all discussing their offshore visits to London, Its weather, food etc. Avani was going to see her dream destination for the first time! The cab arrived at the airport. They saw her off at the departure gate. It was time for Avani to leave the sight of her existing world and turn towards her professional world. It was a liberating feeling! She felt as if courage and confidence were inviting her with open arms. She checked in her luggage and was waiting for an immigration check. An old South Indian lady was playing some crossword game on her cell phone. That caught Avani's attention. She had another 45 minutes for an immigration check. She felt like voluntarily talking to that old lady. Avani went and sat beside her. That old lady smiled at Avani with a friendly guesture and introduced herself "I am Sumati, I am going alone to London to meet my friend. From there, we both roam around Europe to see places". Avani felt so delighted. Avani also introduced herself and said that she was going to a conference.

That old lady looked older than Vedavalli. She was so active and enthusiastic! Avani got caught in her enthusiasm. She wanted to know more. Sumati was also getting too bored at the immigration counter and she was also longing for a company to talk to. So she started talking about herself. "I am 72 years old now. It was my dream to see Europe. I lost my husband last year. I stay with my son and daughter-in-law. My daughter-in-law is carrying for the second time. She is expecting a baby in another 15 days. I told my son that I wanted to go and meet my childhood friend Mythili. She has been calling me and telling me that she will accompany me on a Europe tour. She has been staying there for two decades and knows the places around very well. Avani was surprised to hear about her and asked "Aunty, your daughter-in-law will be delivering the baby and you don't want to be here?" Sumati smiled and said "I have lived life for others' sake too much. Now I think I need to pause and understand that even without me life will move on. Before I leave this world, I want to travel, rather travel with a light heart, have some happy moments and exit. Avani was stunned at her view! She asked, "sorry for a personal question , but are you not comfortable with your daughter-in-law?" Sumati smiled and said" It is all in the mind. I am comfortable with her. She has some expectations of me. I am not that. Rather, I don't want to be that. I am a very fun-loving person. I need music, people, stories and lots of positive vibes around me. I can never work like a timetable. I have a creative way of doing things. But my daughter-in-law has a different set of expectations from me. She feels I should be a disciplined homemaker which will fit the definition of an elderly woman taking care of home. She feels I am inefficient in managing my home. She was right. Then I started figuring out that I never wanted to be a homemaker! She introduced me to myself! So, I am stepping aside so her journey is smooth. This time she wanted only her mother's help and not mine. It was an eye-opener for me that she is helping me to focus on myself and offering my me-time back to me! When my elder granddaughter was born, I took care of my daughter-in-law and the kid. I felt I was a superwoman. Cooking all possible healthy recipes, and taking the best care of the kids, in the process, I never realized that my excess love and concern was suffocating them. In the process of taking care of her, I neglected my health. I fell sick. Later in a hard way, I realized that all are adults and they can take care. Even if they are our children. I realized one thing Avani, If people need help, They will ask. If we feel it is within our limits and we can do some value addition by helping them, only then we must offer the help. Else we need to pull back. Attaching all emotions to it, we will be troubling ourselves and also others. Sometimes, not intruding in others' path is also a help! "Avani felt it was so true. Sumati said " I have kept my best sarees for the trip and also I had bought two nice sets of trousers and tops, Which I had exclusively kept to wear for my husband's 75th birthday and surprise him. But fate had different plans". Avani could see the tears in Sumati's eyes. Immediately Sumati could hide the tears with her smile and said "But he is there with me forever. I have taken those dresses for my trip. I want the best photos of mine in these dresses in a nice background, we are also planning to sing and dance! I want to live my life to the fullest on this trip". Avani got goosebumps seeing the spirit of Sumati. She felt overjoyed. She gave a gentle hug to Sumati and wished her a happy and safe trip. Immigration check started and both Sumati and Avani boarded the plane. Their seat numbers were two rows away from each other. The plane took off and the airlift helped Avani to lose the gravity of her guilt behind!

As the plane descended through the clouds, the sprawling city of London emerged beneath, its iconic landmarks dotting the landscape like miniature pieces of a grand puzzle. Avani was excited and the hum of excitement filled her heart as the plane touched down at Heathrow Airport.

Stepping off the plane, a wave of diverse accents and languages enveloped her, a testament to London's international allure. The air, crisp and cool, hinted at the adventures awaiting beyond the airport gates. A glance out the terminal window revealed the unmistakable red double-decker buses navigating the airport lanes and the distant silhouette of the London Eye against the skyline. She saw Sumati at a distance and she bid bye to her and wished her a nice trip. She could spot a chauffeur carrying a nameplate of her name. It was the conference team that had sent a cab. Avani went by the cab to her accommodation.

Embarking on her maiden professional trip, Avani found herself in awe as she stepped into a London hotel. The blend of contemporary elegance and cultural nuances left her mesmerized. The well-appointed room, adorned with modern amenities, contrasted with a sense of warmth that made her feel at home. As she navigated the intricacies of the hotel, the cosmopolitan atmosphere and diverse clientele fueled her excitement. The international setting, coupled with the flawless service, offered a unique blend of comfort and adventure. The experience of staying in a London hotel for the first time became a memorable chapter in her professional journey, adding a global perspective to her travels.

The next morning, Avani got dressed up in her neat handloom cotton saree which spoke about India's rich artistic handloom skill and culture. She knotted her long hair which was suiting her very well. She came down to the breakfast buffet hall where she could see many people who were ready to attend the conference. She was welcomed personally by Arundhati Roy, Head of Dept of Ecology and Environment, Govt of Karnataka. She introduced Avani to some more speakers and eminent scientists. It was an excellent exposure to Avani.

She walked through the sprawling campus of ***Central Hall Westminster***. Central Hall Westminster located in the heart of London, looked like a grand and historic venue surrounded by an expansive and well-maintained campus. The impressive campus encompassed elegant gardens and open spaces that provided a tranquil setting amid the bustling city. The iconic Central Hall building itself was like a masterpiece of architectural brilliance, featuring majestic facades and intricate detailing. The sprawling grounds offered a combination of landscaped gardens, pathways, and charming courtyards, creating a welcoming environment for visitors. The well-manicured lawns and lush greenery add a touch of natural beauty to the surroundings. Avani was delighted to see the campus.

Avani was the third speaker at the conference. It was her turn and her name was called. She had two options. Either to allow the moment to define her or to grab the moment and define it! She embraced the opportunity to showcase her capabilities at a prestigious London conference. As she stepped onto the international podium, her poised demeanour and articulate presentation immediately captured the audience's attention. Dressed beautifully in a blend of traditional Indian attire and modern professionalism, she effortlessly blended cultural richness with global competence. Her eloquent speech, coupled with insightful perspectives, not only demonstrated her expertise but also transcended cultural boundaries. The way she presented the data points on the rich western ghats of Karnataka and the way the plastic pollution was a threat to western ghats and in turn how it was impacting the global environment was truly remarkable. The audience, initially unaware of her presence, was left astounded by her confidence and proficiency, challenging stereotypes and leaving an unforgettable mark on the London conference.

After the conference ended, it was a fulfilling experience for Avani. She had a day left to spend at the hotel. She decided to venture alone on a guided city tour of London. It was the first time; she had made this independent decision! Her cell phone rang and it was Mr. Iyengar on the phone "Avani, The little one has fallen sick. Yesterday the whole night he had a high fever. Wanted to ask you which medicine to give?". The mother in Avani surfaced and the guilt also surfaced! She told about the medicines that need to be given. Then she asked if Srini was around. They said he had gone out for some bank work. Unlike the other times, Avani chose peace over guilt! For a moment she paused and said to herself "After I came over here, Kid falling sick is out of my control. I know he is in safe hands. Let me pray with faith for his speedy recovery. Am sure it will be viral fever and will subside in a day or two. This is the only day available for me to explore the place. If I sulk here worrying in a hotel room, it's more depressing. Let me just move out. For a moment Avani felt, a stranger had come out from inside of her! She looked into her eyes in the mirror of the dressing table in her room. She was happy to see the confident version of herself! She said to herself, City of London, Avani is coming to see you"!

Venturing into the bustling streets of London for the first time on a professional trip, an Indian woman found herself immersed in the vibrant tapestry of the city's rich history and contemporary allure. As she embarked on a guided city tour, the iconic landmarks unfolded before her, each narrating a tale of its own. The juxtaposition of historic architecture and modern skyscrapers left her in awe, reflecting the city's dynamic spirit. The red double-decker buses, the quintessential black cabs, and the river Thames meandering through the urban landscape created a sensory symphony that resonated with cultural diversity. The allure of Buckingham Palace, the timelessness of Big Ben, and the cosmopolitan vibe of Covent Garden collectively painted a vivid picture of London's multifaceted charm. Avani felt a sense of exhilaration and cultural enrichment, making her first experience of the city a memorable chapter in her professional journey. She closed her eyes in front of the London tower bridge, which she had seen through her grandfather's description of Wordsworth's poetries. She imagined her best childhood imagination of seeing London with her grandfather. For a moment she felt he was there with her, experiencing the beauty of London in the same way as her! She shopped a few souvenirs in a small shop near Tower bridge. As the evening set in, Avani returned to the hotel and felt too refreshed in mind, despite being physically tired.

The next day, she left for the airport. This was the most thrilling trip of her life. As she boarded the flight back home, a profound sense of fulfilment enveloped her. The memories of the bustling city, the successful conference, and the enriching cultural experiences lingered in her mind, casting a warm glow over the journey. Sitting in the aircraft, she reflected on the personal and professional growth achieved during the trip. The anticipation of reuniting with people at Iyengar mansion added a touch of joy to her heart. The aerial view of London bidding farewell, combined with the realization of a successful venture, evoked a sense of accomplishment. With a heart full of gratitude and a newfound appreciation for international experiences, she looked forward to returning home, carrying with her the lessons and memories from this transformative London trip. She had loads and loads of her experience to share with her people at the Iyengar mansion She was already missing home and was eager to see her kids. From the airport, just before boarding the flight, she called up home and found out that the little one's fever had subsided and he was okay. Vedavalli asked over the phone "Avani, how was London? "Avani said, "London was awesome, but I am missing your homemade rasam" Vedavalli was on cloud nine and a mother's affection arose in her.She said "you come home. I will keep it ready for you".

The next day afternoon, the flight landed and Avani boarded a cab and went home. Kids came running to her. She hugged the Children. Srini helped her to keep the luggage inside. Mr. Iyengar who had kept a count of Avani's luggage while she left, was counting them to cross-check and verify, to ensure all luggage was safe. The little one was already eager to see the bus and car as souvenirs that Avani had got for him. Vedavalli gave her instructions to put the luggage in Sun, wash the clothes, take a shower and only later she could enter the kitchen! Avani's London flight in mind completely landed on the ground with Vedavalli's stern instructions! At home, Mr. and Mrs. Iyengar kept everyone's egos in check and ensured all were grounded.

6

Harmony Found!

"Balancing family and career is like conducting an orchestra; it requires skill, patience, and a deep understanding of each instrument's role. When done right, it creates a masterpiece"

– Anonymous

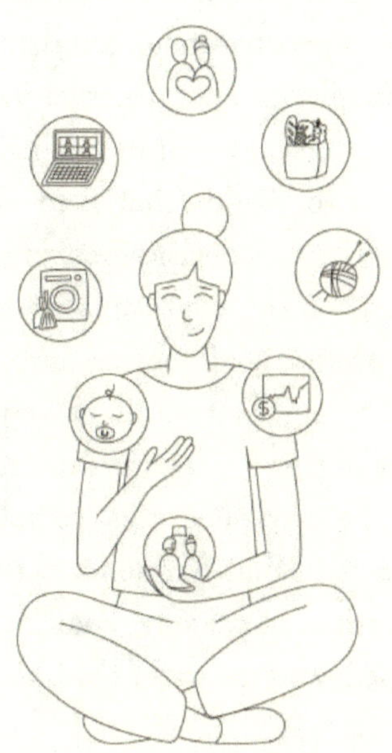

It was a scorching summer, of March. Children's exams and study stress had percolated even to parents. Avani felt the need to be more available for her children during their formative years. Believing that spending more time would support both their academics and co-curricular activities, she decided to resign from her job in February. All the scientists around her criticized her decision and some advised her that she was spoiling her career by making such a bad decision. But Avani had a firm mind. She felt she should be available for kids around their exam time. The office was not ready to let go of her services. So, she agreed to do a part-time job, in which she insisted that she preferred to work from home till the children's exams were over.

Caught in the intricate web of responsibilities, Avani always found herself grappling with the overwhelming dilemma of prioritizing between her flourishing career and the demands of her family. In the perpetual juggle of meetings, deadlines, and the constant pull of familial ties, she always felt torn between two worlds that held equal significance in her life. The weight of decision-making was becoming a formidable burden, as she contemplated the impact of her choices on both professional success and the well-being of her loved ones. This internal conflict always evoked a sense of confusion in balancing personal aspirations and familial obligations. As she navigated this complex maze, Avani sought to carve a path that harmonized her ambitions and the emotional fabric of her family, knowing that the choices made would shape the narrative of her life.

At Iyengar Mansion, Mr. and Mrs. Iyengar were in a different world. Summer was festive for them as Vedavalli used to look for the fierce Sun to prepare papads and pickles for the entire year! In the scorching heat of the Bangalore summer, the air filled with the amazing aroma of spices at Iyengar mansion as Vedvalli joyously embarked on the tradition of making papads and pickles. With a twinkle in her eyes and a contagious enthusiasm, she sat amidst an array of vibrant spices, sun-dried lentil wafers, and a medley of fresh vegetables. The rhythmic pounding of mortar and pestle resonated through the kitchen as she skillfully ground and mixed ingredients, infusing each creation with the warmth of her seasoned hands and a lifetime of culinary wisdom. Vedavalli's excitement was so evident as she recollected tales of bygone summers, reminiscing about the joy these homemade delicacies brought to her family. She believed that this cherished tradition not only preserves flavours but also becomes a heartwarming celebration of heritage, connecting generations through the timeless pleasure of savouring homemade delights crafted with love.

This intense passion of Vedavalli was too much for Avani to handle as Avani used to be her assistant in all these ventures. Since Shreeja was in a corporate job, she could not give time for elaborate culinary protocols of Vedavalli. She used to help when time permitted over weekends. But Avani was a passionate cook and she was always eager to learn the art and science of cooking and kitchen management. But in Vedavalli's kitchen, Avani was always a shadow despite her talents and interests. Avani used to love learning the culinary skills from Vedavalli which used to be accurate and reproducible like science experiments. But the only catch was that Vedavalli was a perfectionist and always wanted things her way only. She never used to encourage Avani's innovative and less cumbersome way of cooking.

Though both these ladies had a passion for cooking, their frequencies never matched. In the heart of her middle years, Avani had rediscovered a fervent passion for culinary exploration. Fueled by an unquenchable curiosity and a desire to infuse innovation into the mosaic of tradition, she had boarded on a culinary journey to master and reinvent traditional recipes. With a gleam in her eyes and a stack of treasured family cookbooks as her guide, she used to immerse herself in the art of cooking with infectious enthusiasm. She used to consider each day as an opportunity for experimentation, blending time-honoured techniques with a creative twist. For her, kitchen was a vibrant laboratory where aromas of spices and the sizzle of pans were meant to recite a tale of culinary exploration. She used to transform the dining table into a canvas, showcasing her culinary creations as she proudly presented reinvented traditional dishes, beautifully plated and bursting with flavours that bridged the gap between heritage and contemporary flair. Avani's zest for learning and passion for cooking become a testament to the timeless joy of reinventing tradition with a touch of innovation.

Her energy used to be punctured when Vedavalli used to come out with a broad spectrum of instructions on dos and don'ts. In the dynamic dance of these family relationships, a clash of contrasting personalities emerged as a perfectionist and non-innovative Vedavalli encountered her enthusiastic and innovative daughter-in-law Avani. Vedavalli rigidity in her steadfast pursuit of perfection, viewed traditional ways as sacred and she remained resistant to any deviation. But Avani, brimming with creativity and with a fondness for innovation, always introduced new and imaginative approaches to cooking or household management due to which she always met with disrespectful snubs. Vedavalli's rigid standards and reluctance to embrace change created an atmosphere of disapproval, leaving Avani disheartened.

Not only in Iyengar Mansion, but this is a case with every household. Such clashes highlight the challenge of bridging generation gaps and the struggle for acceptance in a household where tradition and innovation engage in a subtle tug-of-war. Avani's resilience, however, used to be a beacon of hope, as she always navigated this complex relationship with the determination to find common ground, fostering a delicate balance between respecting tradition and embracing the potential for positive change.

Avani, with a lot of interest and passion used to learn and prepare papads and pickles and all the other traditional cuisines along with Vedavalli. Very few could recognize her passion. Many of her friends used to make fun of her as a twelfth-century woman as she was indulging in age-old practices. Many of her colleagues used to mock at her and used to comment that she was giving time for unproductive things being a scientist. One of her senior bosses at her office, Dr Savithri had commented "Come on Avani, grow up. All these pickles, papads and spice powders are available in abundance in the market. Why do you need to spend time on these things unnecessarily? Instead, why don't you give more time for your career?" All such comments made Avani a selective introvert as she felt it was unnecessary to prolong a discussion or explain to people who never understood her views.

Caught between the traditional notions of homemaking held by her mother-in-law and the modern, free-willed ideals endorsed by her professional colleagues, she found herself at a crossroads. The clash of these contrasting viewpoints fostered a sense of inner turmoil, leaving her torn between the conventional responsibilities tied to home and family and the desire to pursue personal and professional aspirations. Struggling to strike a balance, she sought a middle path that aligned with her values and aspirations. She had so many unanswered questions to herself. She had a scientific temper with a traditional bent of mind which made her enjoy the art and science of home making protocols.

While Avani sent her kids to exams and was lost in some thoughts, she heard Vedavalli "Avani, quickly spread a mat on the terrace. We will spread this lentil dough and put it for drying. Later, from the fresh lemons I have washed and wiped in the kitchen, we will make pickles today. I have told your father-in-law to bring the chilli powder. Last time he bought some local variety as he was too lazy to go far to our regular grocery store. So, this time I have told him strictly to buy the good quality stuff from there." Avani got tagged with Vedavalli. It was a package offer for Avani. Only if she tolerated the rigid instructions from Vedavalli, she get to learn the amazing recipes as a gift. That was the reason she always signed up for it. Learning amidst odds is not just about acquiring knowledge; it's about cultivating resilience, determination, and an unbreakable spirit

As Vedavalli and Avani were preparing papads, on the next house terrace, a post-middle-aged woman, wearing sunglasses, track-pant and a t-shirt, also came to spread the papads on the terrace. Behind her, her husband also came along holding a vessel containing papad dough, to help his wife. Vedavalli gave a smile hiding her sarcastic look with very great difficulty. Vedavalli called Avani and introduced her new neighbour. "Avani, she is our new neighbour, Sahana. They moved in last week. I met her yesterday while shopping for vegetables from the cart vendor in front of the house". Sahana smiled at Avani and said " Hai Avani, nice meeting you. My husband and myself have relocated to this home from Mumbai. Meet my husband Sundareshan. Avani smiled and was glad to meet that couple. In her first impression, they looked very smiling and friendly. Sahana told Avani "I saw your kids. The other day, while they were playing cricket, a ball fell on our balcony and we helped them to get it. I heard from your mother-in-law that you are a scientist. Good to know". Avani asked, "How about your family?" Sahana continued "We have two sons. One stays abroad. He got married last month and moved back to America. My second son is in Mumbai and in a month, he will be moving to Australia for pursuing his master's degree. So, we both are starting our retired life in Bangalore. Please do drop in the evening for a cup of coffee. Will wait for you. I don't know anyone around. Am yet to get used to this new home and new place." Avani felt Sahana was very pleasant and friendly to interact with. She said she would surely come for coffee at Sahana's house. After they left, Vedavalli passed a comment. "Making flawless traditional papads needs a lot of dedication and focus. Everyone can't do it". Avani got the intent of Vedavalli's judgmental pulse. Vedavalli continued, "that Sahana looks quite smart. She is getting her husband to do her work of making papads!"

Avani interrupted "Amma, please stop interpreting things. She might not look as traditional as you are but she might be good at making papads and she might like doing them so she is doing it. Maybe not because she HAS to do it! She and her husband are working together as a team. What is wrong with that? Who said making papads is only ladies' job?!" Vedavalli said "I can get the pulse of people quickly. I have seen these stylish ladies. These people are not so home-oriented and not so hard-working. I would have never told my husband to do papads! The home-bent people have a different charm. You belong to this generation. You won't understand." Avani could not, rather was not interested to continue this gossipy talk anymore. Both of them spread the lentil papads and went down to the kitchen to make pickles.

Pickle preparation started in the kitchen. The aromatic fresh lemons, chillies, and ginger were ready to unite with spices! As the aroma of spices wafted through the air, Vedavalli sat down with Avani, in the cosy kitchen. With a gentle but firm tone and tenor, she began sharing her perspective on homemaking. She spoke of the time-honoured traditions that had been passed down through generations, emphasizing the importance of patience, dedication, and the nurturing touch required to create a harmonious home. Vedavalli, who had spent decades perfecting the art of homemaking, expressed her concern about the modern career-centric lifestyle, stating that the rapid pace and constant demands often left individuals ill-equipped to manage the intricate balance of a household. She recalled the joy of weaving family bonds through shared meals and cherished rituals, lamenting that the essence of homemaking seemed to be fading in the face of contemporary priorities.

Avani, a career-oriented woman with a heart full of aspirations, listened respectfully but couldn't help but feel a twinge of conflict within. As Vedavalli spoke, Avani recognized the wisdom in her mother-in-law's words but also pondered the value of pursuing personal ambitions. The generation gap was evident, and amidst the clinking of traditional cookware, Avani was lost in finding her balance between the timeless wisdom of her mother-in-law and the evolving demands of the modern world.

That evening, Avani abided by the invite, got ready and went to Sahana's home for coffee. Sahana opened the door and welcomed her with a warm smile. She was dressed in a beautiful handloom cotton saree. She had worn glass bangles and a string of jasmine fell across her plat looking very beautiful. Avani complimented her "Wow you look beautiful!" Sahana thanked her for the compliment and took Avani inside her home. Avani got lost inside. Sahana's house with a rustic and spiritual taste emanated a serene and soulful ambiance. Earthy tones dominated the interiors, with warm terracotta and muted greens adorning the walls. Traditional wooden furniture, intricately carved with artistic motifs, complemented the overall aesthetic. The living space featured a modest yet cosy prayer corner adorned with brass lamps, aromatic incense, and idols of deities. A large wooden open bookshelf hosting an array of books, and textured fabrics in natural fibers, like cotton and jute, added a tactile dimension to the decor. A small meditation nook, with comfortable floor cushions and soft lighting, invited moments of contemplation. The air was filled with the soothing notes of devotional music, creating a tranquil atmosphere that reflected Sahana's spiritual connection and appreciation for simplicity. Avani said "Your home looks so beautiful! This is exactly my taste!"

While they were talking, Sundareshan, Sahana's husband, came from the kitchen holding two coffee mugs. The aroma of the freshly brewed and blended coffee wafted through the entire house and competed with the fragrance of flowers and incense sticks! He offered both of them the fresh filter coffee and said "Hello beautiful ladies, here is your coffee". He turned towards Sahana and gave a naughty smile and said, "Madam, your cook is seeking permission to go out for an evening walk. Can I go?" Sahana with a smiling eye, said "please stop bugging me and go and please go for a long walk and come late." He turned towards Avani and said, "Avani, it is excellent to have you with us. Please feel at home and all the best to you as you are getting trapped with Sahana! I am also going out for an evening walk. If you need any help, I will share my cell phone number. If you need a headache balm at the end of the conversation with Sahana, am at your service. Will surely bring it." Sahana, hiding her laughter, showed the false anger in her eyes and showed him the way towards the door. Avani felt very happy to see their friendly interaction.

Sahana called Avani to rest on a stone bench next to the bay window in the dining hall. There a big family group photo caught Avani's eyes. The traditional costumes of the elders reflected the orthodox background as well. Sahana saw questioning eyes of Avani and introduced her big joint family, her in-laws, her three elder brothers-in-law, their wives, their children and also a third-generation family cook at the end of the pic. Avani, with a shine in her eyes, said, " I want to know more about you. It was an instant connection as soon as I saw you!" Sahana acknowledged Avani's friendly compliment with a smile and said that she worked as a scientist at Bhabha Atomic Research Centre, Molecular Biology division in Mumbai and took voluntary retirement as she felt her family needed her more at that time. Avani was surprised. She said, "Wow you served as a scientist there? How could you manage this big family and a career? I am dumb stuck! I find it so hard to strike a balance between my work and family! I have so many unanswered questions for myself."

Sahana recounted her remarkable journey of successfully balancing the intricate tapestry of a large, orthodox South Indian Brahmin joint family, that too in a cosmopolitan city like Mumbai with a thriving career as a molecular biology scientist. She explained how she had to balance the cooking in a kitchen with so many ladies! She said her sisters-in-law were also like her mother-in-law as she was youngest! How she used to handle everything with a smile, sneak in, and finish her schedules to be off to work!". Avani was surprised!

Her narrative sounded like a testament to resilience and determination, where traditional values and modern aspirations harmoniously coexist. She spoke with grace about navigating familial expectations while pursuing her passion, highlighting moments of compromise, adaptation, and unwavering commitment. The way her mother-in-law took control over others and the way their sisters-in-law used to express indifference as only Sahana was a working daughter-in-law. The way she had to manage work in the lab when children fell sick, the way she struggled to save her leaves for her family functions. Her eyes lit up as she described the silent and constant support of her husband, the joy of breaking stereotypes and fostering a supportive environment at home.

Avani was taken aback! She asked "Did you never feel guilty or torn between two worlds? Sahana said "Of course I felt. Sometimes it was so hard that my husband was like my punch bag. I used to vent all silly tantrums of helplessness and anger on him! But he stood like a lighthouse for me showing my direction and purpose. He always used to say Stop pleasing others Sahana and stop seeking their validation. You are working as a scientist, as it is your passion and you cannot and need not explain it to others. It is my duty to support you and at the same time, it is our duty to stand by the family when they need us. With different people of different mindsets together, it will create diverse opinions. You need not fight all your battles. You will find a way out when your intentions are correct and your efforts are honest and sincere. This advice of him was my torchlight in my professional and personal journey. I stayed in a joint family till my elder son completed his under graduation. Later, after my in-laws passed away, all the families moved into nuclear families. After my sons have settled, now we both have moved here. So, this is my story in a nutshell Avani." She gently looked at Avani and smiled. The tale unfolded as a rich mosaic of achievement, showcasing the symbiotic relationship between family bonds and professional accomplishments, leaving Avani inspired to forge her path.

Avani opened up "Sometimes, how much ever I struggle to be good at balancing home and office, I feel I am not good enough. I can never get approval from my mother-in-law who is obsessed with her perfect protocols of doing things nor I can withstand her nagging. At the office, though I get the best working zeal and encouragement, I can never stick there due to guilt. From managing household chores to attending school functions and office meetings, I struggle to navigate a constant ebb and flow between two worlds. The struggle lies not only in the physical demands but also in the emotional toll of meeting expectations on both fronts." Avani was almost in tears as her hidden pain was surfacing.

Sahana patted her back and said " It is not easy to wade through in a joint family. But remember, the more chisels the stone takes, the more intricate and beautiful the statue it can become! Try to be wise and pull back when you have no control over situations. DETACH is the answer. Many Mothers-in-law usually dominate as they feel the insecurity for power inside. They would have suffered it in their times due to the dominating male heads of the family. Especially in previous generations, women did not even have financial independence or when they see efficient daughters-in-law, they get scared that they might lose their power. At the same time, when we run too much behind careers, it's a vicious cycle. Money and power start ruling us and it is a different level of insecurity. We lose very precious and beautiful moments of life. The secret is to keep calm and know that you are playing roles and your identity is beyond this.

Darling, life is a beautiful tapestry woven with the threads of both career and family. It is not about choosing one over the other; it is about finding harmony between the two. Embrace the ebb and flow of each role, knowing that there will be times when one takes precedence over the other. Don't be too hard on yourself; perfection is an illusion. Prioritize what truly matters, delegate when you can, and savour the precious moments with your loved ones. Your journey is unique, and there's no 'one-size-fits-all' approach. Trust your instincts, stay true to your values, and remember that the most meaningful achievements often unfold when you strike a balance that feels right for you and your family." Avani gave a friendly hug to Sahana and was about to leave and there Sundareshan returned from his evening walk. He asked Avani, "hope you both had a good time. Oh! I forgot to get the pain balm!" Avani said, "Certainly no need for any pain balm. It was so nice to talk to her.Her talk itself was a balm for my confused mind. I was amazed listening to her multi-tasking in her life story". Immediately, Sundareshan gave a proud look at Sahana and said, "Avani, I am proud of her achievements. I wonder sometimes how she manages so much!" The wholehearted appreciation of a wife from her husband sounded extremely wonderful to Avani. Sundareshan continued "As the head of a cutting-edge research project, she had determined to secure funding for her groundbreaking work in molecular Biology. But her meticulously planned day would unravel into a series of challenges.

I want to tell you about one instance Avani, As usual, Sahana was already in her home laboratory, reviewing her project proposal one last time before the crucial presentation later that day. That was a special day for our family – As my father Ramanan, was celebrating his 70th birthday. The house buzzed with excitement as relatives from near and far gathered for the occasion. Sahana was stressed to strike a balance. I was also stuck in the office that day and I feel guilty for it even now. I had an urgent meeting at the office, leaving Sahana to manage the birthday preparations. Our son, Arjun, an aspiring young athlete, had a crucial sports tournament scheduled for the same day. With Sahana's packed schedule, it seemed impossible to be present for every important event. Her resilience was put to the test. She juggled between coordinating the birthday celebrations, cheering for Arjun at his sports tournament, and making sure her project proposal was pitch-perfect. The pressure mounted, and it seemed like the universe conspired against her. Amid the chaos, I called Sahana to apologize for my absence and promised to make it up to her later. Determined not to let the circumstances dampen her spirits, Sahana drew strength from within. With the support of family (which she assumed), she managed to delegate tasks, ensuring the birthday festivities proceeded smoothly. As the clock ticked closer to the project presentation, Sahana rushed to the venue, armed with a mind full of scientific brilliance and a heart full of love for her family. The investors were captivated by her passion and the potential impact of her research.

Despite the hurdles, Sahana's dedication shone through, leaving a lasting impression. Back home, our family gathered to celebrate dad's 70th birthday. Sahana, with a sense of accomplishment, joined the festivities, her family's smiles reflecting the strength and resilience that defined her. You know Avani, In the days that followed, news of Sahana's successful project funding spread, and our family cherished the memory of that eventful day. My Dr. Sahana became an inspiration not just in the world of science but also within her own family, proving that with determination and a supportive network, one could conquer even the most challenging situations."

Avani was overwhelmed by the couple. The post-middle-aged couple had an endearing warmth that instantly enveloped anyone in their presence. Their shared laughter and easy-going nature painted a picture of a deep, enduring companionship. In their cosy home, a welcoming haven, the atmosphere was infused with the sound of shared stories. The gentle lines etched by time on their faces told tales of shared joys and weathered challenges, while their affectionate gestures and shared glances revealed a love that had only deepened with the years. Avani felt as if their hospitality knows no bounds, and their genuine interest in others can create a space where friendships naturally flourish. From the bottom of her heart, Avani felt that this friendly couple embodied the beauty of long-lasting love and the kind of warmth that can leave a lasting impression on all fortunate enough to cross their path.

Amidst the whirlwind of confusion about conflicting priorities, Avani found solace in the wisdom of Sahana who pitched in as an efficient mentor. With a gentle smile, the way that seasoned woman shared insights forged through decades of experience. Her advice echoed like a comforting melody, emphasizing the importance of balance in life's intricate symphony. Avani, reassured by the assurance that finding equilibrium is a lifelong quest, felt a weight lift off her shoulders. The simplicity of the counsel – to navigate the delicate dance of life with patience and intentional choices – sounded like a guiding beacon amid chaos, providing Avani with the confidence to chart her path with a newfound sense of clarity and purpose.

7
Self-Worth vs Net Worth

"A woman's worth is not determined by her possessions but by the richness of her soul and the depth of her wisdom."

Financial independence for women these days is like oxygen for life. Immaterial of the technological advancements and cosmopolitan surroundings we are in, at one phase of life, the dilemma faced by many middle-aged women in balancing financial independence and family responsibilities is a multifaceted challenge influenced by societal and family expectations and personal aspirations. On one hand, these women when they are well educated and skilled in various fields, often desire to achieve financial independence and pursue career aspirations, seeking fulfillment and empowerment beyond traditional family roles. Economic independence not only provides a sense of self-worth but also offers greater control over personal decisions and lifestyle choices. Middle-aged women may feel pressure to prioritize family duties such as caregiving for children, and elderly parents, or managing household responsibilities. This can often conflict with career ambitions and hinder their pursuit of financial independence. I think this is not only seen in India but it is a global conflict amongst middle-aged women. Can a woman have it all, a fulfilled career life and a regret-free family life? Are they mutually exclusive?

Avani was no exception to the list of women who underwent this dilemma. She had decided to pursue a part-time research consultation job instead of a full-time job as she had prioritized family needs over her career. It was a Friday afternoon when she was scrolling through her mailbox when she received an e-mail from her close friend Mahima. Avani, Mahima and Jyothsna were very close pals who studied together in high school, undergrad and postgraduation at the university.

Avani was amazingly delighted to receive the mail from her closest pal Mahima. They were like one soul dwelling in two bodies. They were 3 am friends. Mahima had mailed Avani that she was tired of her busy life in New York and she had taken a long break of three months on loss of pay and had so many things on her bucket list. She said the first thing on her bucket list was to meet her college buddies and go on at least a three-day trip. So, she requested Avani to plan. She also said she had informed Jyothsna about it and Jyothsna replied that she would discuss it with family and revert back.

Though Avani was super excited with the idea, always a remote hindrance used to block the spring of her enthusiasm. She wanted to share the news with Srini. By that time Srini called her and said, "Avani, all school fees of kids have been paid and please make a checklist of all payments of medical insurance premiums of all of the family members. Also, we need to divert some funds for some religious ceremonies at the native that Appa is planning. Also, for the upcoming Ugadi festival, need to allocate some money for buying new clothes for all. Appa and Amma were also having heated arguments with the housemaid yesterday when she asked for a salary hike. After you requested, even I thought about it. For the work she is doing, let us pay her extra. You pay her five hundred rupees more this month, please do not mention that to Appa and Amma. They will again organize a civil court at home. You need to be a little prudent on the financial management this month as there is too much of expenditure. Just wanted to discuss that".

Avani's excitement about the trip with her best buddies got locked in her throat and failed to come out. Avani was too shy a person when it came to money matters. Though she managed the house, she never claimed to be the queen of her husband's financial resources. May be since Mr. And Mrs. Iyengar never retired from the finance department of the house and Mr. Iyengar proclaimed himself to be Srini's financial advisor, she never felt that freedom. Always she suffered from a dilemma deep down in her heart, as to what to choose; Deep home-bound quality care for the family or complete financial freedom by choosing a serious career path, compromising the quality of family care by outsourcing to cooks and maids. The second option was fictitiously in her imagination and was never even vocally discussed as an option loudly in the family in Mr. and Mrs. Iyengars' Nazi world of rules and regulations! Avani and Srini had a very silent understanding between them in financial management at home. One used to buffer the other's needs by complementing each other. But somehow, Avani had a strong feeling inside that if she was a career-oriented person and if a job paid her bills, she would have that financial freedom as she would not have to depend on anyone.

But Srini always used to convince her that the way she was keeping everything and everyone intact at home was truly priceless and it was way beyond a fat salaried job. All members at home could have a quality life because of the quality time she gives at home. This gratitude expression used to make Avani speechless even though she was not 100%

convinced of this. A silent and constant string of discontent used to strum in her mind's guitar.

So finally, Avani left her mailbox in her laptop open and forgot to log out. She rushed to the kitchen when she heard Vedavalli seeking some assistance in the kitchen. Srini went to help Avani pack her laptop and Mahima's mail caught his eye on screen. He shut the laptop and packed it back. That evening Srini and Avani went for a walk and Srini asked Avani "So when is your girls' trip? What is the plan with Mahima and Jyothsna? Avani gave a surprised look. He smiled and said I think it's since a long time since you went out. You must go. I will manage the show at home. Avani was super happy. Her smile and a sparkle in her eyes expressed it all.

Jyothsna, as soon as she completed under-graduation, got married. She was the first one in Avani's friends circle to get married. She was a very charming girl. She was a happy homemaker. Her daughter was pursuing Medical sciences and her son was doing his Pre University College. Though she was from a well-off family, she never had exposure to a career world as she got married very early. So, she had her own set of strong fears and withdrawals. She was not confident in money matters. In this aspect, she always had an inferiority complex towards managing her finances. She was rich but was not financially empowered.

Mahima was in New York. That was a place where skyscrapers towered over the streets and success was measured in digits and decimals. Mahima was a brilliant investment banker, navigating the fast-paced world of finance with finesse and determination. Her days were consumed by numbers and deals, her nights filled with networking events and corporate dinners. Her husband was also the CEO of a company doing very well. Both of them were extremely successful in their career path. She had a son and a daughter who were academically very successful. Her eldest son was doing his first year of dentistry and her younger daughter was pursuing engineering in University. Since both Mahima and her husband were busy on their career path, she hired a support system, the help of a Creech and maids to bring up her children. Despite her professional achievements, Mahima felt an emptiness gnawing at her soul. No matter how many deals she closed or bonuses she earned, she couldn't shake the feeling that something essential was missing from her life.

Mahima's life seemed picture-perfect from the outside, adorned with designer suits and luxury cars. Yet, beneath the facade of success, a quiet battle raged within her; a battle between her self-worth and her Net worth. It was at that time she thought of her friends with whom she could be herself and with whom she was rest assured that she would not be judged! so this trip plan popped up in her mind.

Finally, all three friends were super happy and excited to catch up and go on a three-day trip. Conference video calls streamed; typical girly discussions popped up. Kashmir has been the place on bucket list of all three since their college days. So, they decided to go to Kashmir. Mahima went a step ahead and booked *Dal Vivanta*, a five-star hotel of the Taj group. Avani and Jyothsna felt a little overwhelmed with accommodation. They both were not women with jobs and their own money on hand. It was not a matter of affordability. It was the attitude of not spending on oneself.

Jyothsna's uncle who was a pandit in the ashram where a statue of peace of Sri Ramanuja was recently established had assured Jyothsna that he would arrange for a good accommodation for them in the ashram. When Jyothsna expressed this to Mahima, Mahima who was a bubbly and frank girl immediately said "Come on! We are not going on a pilgrimage of peace journey. It is okay once in a while you can unwind in a resort. We are going to Taj and don't change the plan". Jyothsna was already imagining the herculean task of taking the no-objection certificate from her family for this trip. Though she was from a well-off family, she had traded her independence and financial freedom for that lifestyle. It was a men's world at her place. Though women were taken care of well, they were ruled even in this advanced time. Jyothsna found it very hard. Finally, Jyothsna convinced all the men in her big joint family. Her husband, father-in-law, her father-in-law's elder brother, her mother-in-law and then with the remaining energy, got ready for the trip.

Avani was hesitant as she was a bit conscious to splurge on herself. When she expressed it to Srini, he said, "it's a good place. Please carry on". Sometimes the fictitious stories of guilt in the mind will make a person withdrawn and shy away, especially when there is no financial independence.

In the excitement of the trip, youth in all three ladies showed up! Mahima started shopping for her upcoming trip. The land of skyscrapers did not look bright anymore when compared to the beautiful Kashmir of her dreams! Jyothsna who was caught up with the busy protocols to maintain a flawless home, started smiling at herself in the mirror. She had forgotten to look in the mirror! Avani started humming all her favourite songs that she used to sing in her college. As the saying goes, ***one of the best ways to make yourself happy in the present is to recall the happy memories of the past.***

Finally, the most awaited day arrived and all three friends decided that they would be meeting each other at Kashmir airport. Mahima flew from New York, Jyothsna from Mumbai and Avani from Bangalore. The respective flights arrived at Kashmir domestic airport in the gap of an hour. All the three ladies were eager to catch up. Mahima was the first to land. Then Avani arrived with her luggage. As soon as she saw Mahima, she jumped out for joy and went and hugged her. Despite the passage of time, the bond forged during their college years remained strong. The prospect of reconnecting with old friends, of picking up where they left off, is immensely exciting. There is a sense of comfort in knowing that, despite the years apart, they can still find common ground and share a deep connection. They were speechless for some time. Then Mahima asked "where is our obedient queen Jyothsna?" Avani said "You have not surprised her; you have shocked her by booking Taj! Poor girl, I know she would have struggled to make it". Mahima said "It is ok, let her break the ice. If not now, When will she?" While they were talking, Jyothsna arrived and came running to her buddies as soon as she saw them.

And gave a hug to both. The first meeting after two decades allowed the three of them to revisit those shared memories, laugh about old jokes, and revel in the familiarity of each other's company. It was a celebration of the enduring bonds forged in youth.

The cab from the hotel was waiting for them with a chauffeur holding nameplate. They boarded the cab and Went towards Dal Vivanta, Taj Hotel in Kashmir. After two decades of separation, the reunion of three college friends was a jubilant occasion, igniting a torrent of nostalgia and joy. Their laughter echoed through the corridors of time as they embarked on a journey to the picturesque hill station of Kashmir. As they wound their way through lush valleys and towering peaks, memories of their youthful escapades flooded back. They recalled shared lovely experiences. Amidst the serene beauty of Kashmir, they rediscovered the essence of their friendship, strengthened by the passage of time. Each moment spent together was a celebration of the enduring bond forged in college days. Those lovely times with hearts full of gratitude and spirits renewed, they vowed to cherish these precious moments forever, knowing that true happiness lies in the company of cherished friends.

Finally, the cab arrived at the Taj. They had an out-of-the-world experience there. They arrive d at Shikaras on Dal Lake, ready to be taken to the resort. The Dal Lake itself was stunning, with its pristine waters reflecting the surrounding snow-capped peaks of the Himalayas. The sight of the lake, with its tranquil waters shimmering under the sunlight, created a mesmerizing backdrop that captivated the three friends. The Dal Lake is famous for its houseboats and shikaras (traditional Kashmiri wooden boats). These colourful and intricately decorated houseboats, floating peacefully on the lake, added a unique charm to the scenery. Meanwhile, shikaris gracefully glided across the water, offering a romantic and traditional mode of transportation. Within the Dal Lake, there were floating gardens called "Rad" or "Rakhs," where vegetables and flowers were cultivated. These floating gardens, along with the vibrant lotus blossoms that dotted the lake's surface, added bursts of colour and vibrancy to the landscape, creating a truly enchanting sight.

The three friends experienced an amazingly warm hospitality at the hotel and they went to their villa accommodation. So, the three freshened up sat for chit chat and opened up their hearts to each other. Beyond the excitement of the reunion itself, it was also an opportunity for reflection. Seeing old friends can prompt introspection, encouraging each person to reflect on their own lives, choices, and accomplishments since their college days. This introspection can be both empowering and inspiring, as they share their respective journeys and support each other's growth. So, each person shared their life's stories. Mahima and Jyothsna spoke a lot while Avani was more of a silent spectator!

Mahima opened up about how after post-graduation she took an interest in banking and shifted her field. It was a dream come true experience for her. She met her soulmate Shekhar there. She said "I felt happiness was knocking on my doors when Shekhar came into my life. He stayed in a big joint family. He said post-marriage if the need arises if I was ready to quit my job. I made it extremely clear to him that I know how to manage my personal and professional life streams separately. So, I don't want to quit my job at any point in time! My financial freedom and identity matter a lot to me. Shekhar was a gentleman to understood my needs. Immediately after the wedding, we planned to go abroad. Initially, we had a lot of time for each other. Later we both started chasing our dreams. We had our first baby Aarya. We were quite excited and we used to walk the tight ropes of both office life and home life with a new baby. Then Anjali the little one entered our lives. Thankfully we got very good daycare centers for them Shekhar was also extremely cooperative I could continue my career path. In fact, because of our hard-pressed office schedules, we could not be a part of any important events at home that took place in India. He couldn't be there for his brother's wedding and even I couldn't be there for my sister Madhuri's wedding. Both side's parents were feeling very bad. My mom was angry at me. But I must say that we have made our lives financially very comfortable so that we can have a hassle-free life. I feel that financially being independent and efficient is extremely important. But life took a different course. During the pandemic of Covid, my dad passed away and I just couldn't come. It was at that time that my mother needed me the most. It hit me very hard. That stumble was an eye-opener for me. I have been chasing my dreams with so much focus and momentum that it is not allowing me to stop. These days, when I turn back, especially after kids leave the nest, my memory pockets look so hollow and scarce. My job took my time away from kids, their growing-up times, their first tip-toed walking, those first words they uttered, I used to silently admire them by logging into my non-stop calls. I could never give them the cultural exposure of my land where I belonged to. Their teenage moments, their friend's circle, we both have hardly shared with them. Now I feel like getting those moments back. But it is too late. They have grown up and they have their ambitions and life ahead of them for them to chase! My best memories stopped when I completed college. We run behind some mirage that we feel will give us happiness forever. Honestly, coming from a middle-class family, to get into a good job earn a name and fame and make lots of money to lead a luxurious life was my dream. But this is such a dream that the closer and closer I get, the farther and farther the destination seems to move. It is an endless journey! Now I feel like going back to the time machine and reliving life by altering my priorities. But it is too late. In the end, it is the choice we make!"

There was a moment of silence in the air. Immediately Mahima controlled her tears from flowing out of her eyes. Avani gave her a gentle hug and patted her back.

Mahima turned towards Jyothsna, "Hey Miss India, our pretty queen, what's up with you? At least Avani used to ping me now and then and I knew a bit as to what was going on in her life. You disappeared like a new moon!" Jyothsna who was always a silent listener since college days, was just the same. After listening to Mahima, she smiled and opened up to share her life's story. "Mahima, whatever you say, you are truly an inspiration. The way you have set a path for yourself is truly amazing. As you all know I was an over-protected kid at my dad's house. My parents' main ambition in life was to keep me comfortable and happy and settle me in a rich home. I was a blindly obedient daughter who always used to believe that whatever my parents thought for me could never go wrong. It had even blinded my reasoning and analytical ability. I got married to Sanketh. He is a very nice man. But his identity is in his family's shadow. It feels like the family is living our life. Compared to the freedom and pampering I had at my mother's place, I felt that it was quite an intruding and chauvinistic family with the label of concern and care. The family's heads, like a panchayath scheme, conduct meetings analyse pros and cons and then decide what courses the children of the family must take. They decide what functions the women of the family must attend to keep up their family prestige. You know they are the scriptwriters of our life! My dream is to have paani-puris in Juhu Beach with my hubby and kids over the weekend. But since my husband is a big man, the servants come and treat him like a king wherever he goes. I am suffocated with this aristocracy. I have become his queen without freedom. Whenever I go shopping, since it is a joint credit card, my husband gets the message and immediately he enquires what I did with the money. I am fed up. I have traded my freedom at the cost of the huge bank balance of the family! When I buy some dresses, he tries to get me around ten dresses at the weekend. I don't know why everything is linked to the narrative called family prestige! The dining table sounds like a conference hall where board meetings take place. Everything is so formal! Can't even breathe". While Jyothsna was telling she broke down to tears. Mahima hugged her and patted her back. She said "are you speechless? Why didn't you retaliate? You deserve to live the life you want. Jyothsna, your situation is like living in the sea but craving for salt in food!" Jyothsna continued "Amma had thoroughly brainwashed me that money was everything in life. I also like a fool nodded and agreed to it. I never used my brain. Sometimes seeking a comfort zone all the time never taking risks and not venturing to pursue your passion, hinder your metamorphosis. We Stay like caterpillars throughout and never evolve into a butterfly! That is what I have learnt from my life. When I see financially independent women, steering their lives independently I feel I always missed the opportunity."

They both looked at Avani and it was Avani's turn. It was sunset and Avani said, "oh my God ! it's evening already! We are lost in our stories. Come let us go around the lake and talk". The Dal Lake is renowned for its spectacular sunsets and sunrises. As the sun dipped below the horizon from behind the mountains, the sky looked as if it was painted in a myriad of colours, casting a magical glow over the entire landscape and turning the scene into a living canvas of beauty. Avani had a vigorous churning of thoughts in her mind after listening to their friends' life stories. Avani said "Life is a beautiful journey and we feel we are the scriptwriters of our lives. We are not. We are walking on the dotted line that destiny has drawn for us. But how we walk that we need to decide. We always feel the other person's life is great but each person knows his or her journey the best. We cannot compare. At least in the case of all three of us, life gave us a choice of if we needed to work or not. But in so many families, girls become the breadwinners and they need to support the families where they do not have any choice." Mahima responded, "True Avani, I know you have always been good at lectures and debates since college days. Once you start speaking, an expert comes out of your mouth! But tell us your story dear".

Avani said "I am married for 20 years to Srini. We stay in a joint family with in-laws and brother-in-law's family. It has its tradeoffs and advantages to stay in a joint family. I have always signed up for a family-oriented life rather than a career-oriented life as I feel, my role as a wife, a mother, and a daughter-in-law comes first and I need to play the role correctly, not to please others, but to be true to my conscious. I have always been mocked at, by many people that being a scientist I have refused to be on a serious career path. I treat my life as the most scientific platform where I perform experiments to get the best results. I feel that during the kids' growing up time I need to give time for them. It is a wrong notion that kids need us. The truth is, we need kids as we need to fulfil our roles towards them for us to feel complete. Life just moves on .We need to keep shifting our gears in different roles relevantly. I have seen the worst rigidity and attachment of my in-laws towards their home and their best efficiency in maintaining the home and keeping the family bond intact as well. So, after going through a journey in a joint family, it is a huge learning process. I have worked in laboratories with research papers and microscopes and have learnt the most scientific ways of preparing papads and pickles from my mother-in-law too. I got to understand the real significance of all festivals and their cultural significance only after marriage. My mother-in-law's rigid discipline made me a good student. I consider a family platform as my university to learn life's lessons. I am happy with my life. By God's grace, all going well".

Mahima replied "Avani, of all the three of us, you have taken the right decision of walking the middle path instead of travelling in extremes. I think you have been there for family at the same time you have pursued your passion. A regret-free life is an asset Avani, In fact whenever I used to see you, I used to feel that you were wasting your precious life and not using your potential to the fullest. But I was wrong Avani". Avani was silent. Mahima said, "girls, it is getting chill outside come let us go for a coffee!" Jyothsna and Mahima moved towards the poolside coffee counters. Avani stood still, gaping at the setting Sun, listening silently to her inner voice.

Avani always had a regret that she had never been able to be financially independent. and did not have financial freedom. But that that day's sunset at Dal Lake, after knowing their friends' stories brought out the bright sun in her mind. She felt deeply that a successful life is that when you turn back, you must never have a regret that you were not there for someone who needed you the most. She strongly felt raising to an occasion and doing your primary duty is a virtue and that is the purpose of life. When it comes to duty, preferences and prejudices have no scope. She now understood the difference between being wealthy and being rich. Being rich is having money. Being wealthy is to have your time with you so you have the freedom to do whatever you like in whatever way you want. It is a thin line we miss seeing usually. She strongly felt that the most valuable thing you can give to someone is not expensive gifts of money, it is your TIME. It is that valuable part of your life you are giving to someone that won't come back to you. But it makes a huge difference in others' life. She felt grateful that she had given that TIME for her family to nurture it. Those happy moments at school with kids, when the kids wanted her to wipe their tears when they wanted help with their project work when Srini wanted her help to take care of the home so he could comfortably manage the office without any mental stress when her in-laws could count on her for any events at home when she could be there for her friends when they needed her shoulders, when she had those ice cream times and chocolate times with her kids and husband, when her mother in law could find a friend in her to share her regrets in life and her difficulties, when her in-laws had ailments and she took care of them like her children, She felt truly grateful for all of that. Once we sign up for a type of life it is purely our choice and we cannot blame others for our life to be in that way. Once we take accountability and own up, the rest of the things will fall into place. And so, with a heart full of gratitude and a soul at peace, Avani embraced the priceless currency of self-worth, knowing that it was far more valuable than all the riches in the world and one's net worth. She came back from her thoughts as she heard Mahima screaming "Avani, come soon we are going for a moonlight boat ride in *Shikaara*"

The three-day trip ended on a happy note and the friends decided to keep meeting more often. True friends add colours to life. As they came out of the rooms near the checkout counter, they saw beautiful snowcapped mountains.

In the distance, the towering peaks of the Himalayas provide a majestic backdrop to the scene. The contrast between the pristine waters of the lake and the snow white of the mountains created a breathtaking panorama that was truly unforgettable. They returned to their homes and routines, recalling the lovely moments they had. This trip was an eye-opener for Avani than just a sightseeing trip with friends.

8

Perfection vs Excellence

OCD is not a disease that bothers; it's a disease that tortures

– John Green

At Iyengar's mansion, there was some serious discussion going on between Mr. and Mrs. Iyengar when Avani returned home from the library. Avani looked at them to listen to some boiling news which she could make out with their expression. Vedavalli started, "Avani, Saroja had called". Avani was excited." So, how is it going in your sister's place? They all must have rested well and back to their routines, right? What does the new bride Radhika say? Did she get adjusted to her new home?" Vedavalli was quiet. Avani could sense that something was wrong. The previous month, Vedavalli's sister Saroja's son Raghu got married in Chennai. His wife Radhika was also from Chennai. In a short span of a month itself, things were not so smooth between Saroja and her new daughter-in-law Radhika. Some silent friction and frequency mismatch had started. Saroja had informed Vedavalli that she would be coming down to Bangalore to stay at the Iyengar mansion for a week for a change. Avani was happy to know that Saroja was coming but felt a little disturbed to know that things were not so smooth between Radhika and Saroja.

Parthasarathy passed a comment in the air, looking into the newspaper, "Women can't get along well in a joint family". Vedavalli was enraged with that statement. She immediately reacted "I am successful in running a joint family. Can't you see? You men put us in all sorts of uncomfortable and choiceless situations and later pass these wreck less comments!" Avani interrupted, "Now please both of you do not fight over this. We do not know what's the issue in their house. Maybe it is some difference of opinion. Let Saroja aunty come down, later we will know. "Mr. Iyengar started, "now the house will be loaded with entertainment. It will be like live TV serials." He gave a sarcastic smile dropped the newspaper on the table and went for a walk. Vedavalli quickly handed over an empty bag to him and said "You are anyway going for a walk without any agenda, bring veggies from the market when you are back from a walk". Parthasarathy grinned, "you are always a giver, giver of the work!" He made a grumpy face, took the bag and walked out. While walking towards the gate he could hear Vedavalli scream from inside " Ensure that the beans you get are tender and not as bad as what you got last time" but Mr. Iyengar could show his fury by banging the gate loudly.

It was Saturday afternoon and Vedavalli finished her cooking of super special cuisines and was eagerly waiting for her sister. In Vedavalli's mind, Saroja was already in victim mode and the consoling story had already started in mind. As she was thinking, the Cab arrived in front of Iyengar mansion and Saroja got down holding a suitcase and three big bags. She cross-checked her luggage thrice and peeped back in the car twice to check if she had missed out anything in the cab. Avani Immediately spotted the Obsessive-compulsive disorder (OCD) tendency in Saroja. She felt it must be hard for Radhika because of this. Avani could empathize as Vedavalli was also slightly inclined to that tendency, though not as intensely as Saroja. Srini and Avani went to help her with her luggage. They welcomed her inside. Avani gave her a gentle hug and asked, "Saroja aunty, how is life after your son's wedding? Saroja gave a blank smile. As soon as she went inside before even greeting others at home she rushed with panic towards the sink and washed her hands thoroughly. Then she could take a sigh of relief. Srini asked "Aunty how is life after Raghu's wedding? "

Saroja could not hold back anymore.Since her son's wedding. Saroja was often finding herself caught in a whirlwind of emotions, oscillating between joy and nostalgia. Amidst the festivities, she couldn't help but recall the days when her son was still under her care, longing for those moments of closeness and dependence. Now, as she navigated through the changes, she couldn't shake off the feeling of emptiness that was creeping in, missing the hustle and bustle of daily interactions. From preparing his favourite dishes to offering advice on life's nuances, she was feeling a subtle shift in their dynamics. Though she had welcomed her daughter-in-law Radhika with open arms, there was a tinge of sadness in realizing that her role had evolved. Despite the occasional cribbing about the changes, she held onto the cherished memories while embracing the new chapter with an open heart, knowing that love and family ties will always remain steadfast.

She said "Srini, Raghu has changed a lot. He has now shifted his life to a new dimension." Sreeja, Vedavalli's elder daughter-in-law interrupted "Exactly that is the intent of marriage!" Saroja said "Radhika is a very sweet and social girl. She has got adjusted to the house but not me." There was a cocktail of sadness, anger and regret in her face. Saroja was an extremely meticulous homemaker. She was a person who was a cleanliness freak and used to keep her house spic and span. She hardly could accept others' ways of working. She looked very social but the fact was she was not a team player at all. Sometimes the image we will be having on ourselves might be opposite to what we are. It needs a lot of courage for unbiased self -introspection. We always feel I am okay and the other person is wrong. To see things from a witness position demands a lot of maturity.

Saroja was a 'go-to person' for help in all situations and even she was very eager to help everyone. But She had an intense tendency of obsessive-compulsive disorder which was often misread by others as perfectionism or hard working! Perfectionism is a self-destructive and addictive belief system that fuels a primary thought that "If I look perfect and do everything perfectly, I can avoid or minimize the painful feeling of shame, judgement or blame". Obsessive Compulsive Disorder is not about cleanliness or perfectionism, it is about fear and Uncertainty!

From the moment Saroja wakes, her mind gets caught in a web of intrusive thoughts, compelling her to meticulously arrange every item in her modest home, aligning them with utmost precision. Her days are punctuated by repetitive rituals, from washing her hands with scalding water to meticulously checking all vessels in the kitchen for dirt or detergent remnants before cooking. Despite the chaos that rages within her mind, Saroja presents a facade of composure to the world, masking her inner turmoil with a serene smile. Yet, behind closed doors, she battles tirelessly against the relentless tide of compulsions, yearning for a resemblance of normalcy amidst the cacophony of her mind.

Vedavalli and Saroja's untiring kitchen discussions started and Avani was startled that Saroja could control and dominate Vedavalli's views! As soon as Saroja entered

Vedavalli's kitchen, she started rearranging all the vessels and convinced Vedavalli that only her way was the most convincing way of arrangement. Vedavalli had the supreme bias due to sibling bond with Saroja because of which she could tolerate Saroja's instructions, else she was not a person who could take feedback about her work from anyone. Avani was seeing all this and just imagined if she had rearranged things in her mother-in-law's kitchen! Saroja started washing all the vessels in the sink and it was like a repeat telecast of washes each time! She started washing her hands frequently and started checking for stains and dirt in the kitchen slab as and when she was talking to Vedavalli. She said a hundred ways in which Vedavalli was going wrong with her kitchen protocols. Avani now understood what was the issue between Saroja and Radhika.

Avani could spot that Saroja's problem needed some psychologist's or if required, medical intervention. But she was a little apprehensive to voluntarily suggest it as she might take it too personally. Avani called up psychologist Dr. Vasantha in Kanakapura, which was outskirts of Bangalore and explained to her about Saroja's condition. Vasantha said, "Avani, why don't you come over? We will talk over lunch?" Avani informed Srini about this, took her car and drove to Kanakapura. It was always a pleasure to meet Dr. Vasantha, as she radiated knowledge and positive vibes. Avani always looked forward to meeting her. She was always attracted to Dr. Vasantha due to her magnetic personality and positive attitude. Vasantha was waiting for Avani at her farm clinic for lunch. They exchanged greetings and Avani expressed her concern about Saroja. Dr. Vasantha took a while and clearly explained "Avani, OCD is a very common psychological disorder today, especially in stressful urban lifestyle. But unfortunately, many suffer from this without knowing the fact that it could be treated. Women are more prone to this condition. One contributing factor may be societal pressures and expectations placed on women, which can lead to heightened levels of stress and anxiety. Women often face numerous roles and responsibilities, including those related to family, career, and social relationships, which can create significant pressure to meet perceived standards of perfection. Additionally, hormonal fluctuations, particularly during pregnancy and postpartum periods, can also trigger or aggravate OCD symptoms in some women. Genetic predisposition, environmental influences, and neurobiological factors may also play a role in the development of OCD. It is essential for individuals experiencing symptoms of OCD to seek professional help and support in managing their condition. However, in some cases, individuals with OCD may exhibit behaviours that appear to treat others as objects or machines due to the nature of their obsessions and compulsions. OCD can manifest in various ways, including an intense need for order, symmetry, or control. This can sometimes lead to individuals with OCD fixating on specific routines or patterns, which may inadvertently affect their interactions with others.

For example, someone with OCD might become excessively focused on a particular task or ritual, such as organizing objects in a certain way or repeatedly checking that doors are locked. In these instances, they may seem preoccupied and less attentive to the needs or feelings of those around them, leading others to feel overlooked or disregarded. It's essential to understand that these behaviours are driven by the individual's internal struggles with anxiety and compulsions, rather than a deliberate intent to dehumanize others. With appropriate treatment and support, individuals with OCD can learn to manage their symptoms and develop healthier coping mechanisms that allow for more empathetic and compassionate interactions with others. Therapy, medication, and support groups are among the resources available to help individuals with OCD lead fulfilling lives while maintaining healthy relationships with those around them. Avani, maybe she has not even introspected that she needs help. If possible, try to find out if she is open for help. Over the age, these traits would have etched strong grooves in their thinking pattern. Will be more difficult to handle if left untreated for an extended period." Avani thanked Dr. Vasantha for the detailed insights she provided about OCD.

She was driving back and, on her way back, she received Radhika's phone. She greeted Radhika and asked how her new life was going on. Radhika said she was in the process of adjusting. She also expressed to Avani that her mother-in-law Saroja was a big challenge to handle and she was finding it very difficult to deal with. She said "it is only a month since I got married, and I am finding it extremely hard to get adjusted to the home Avani. It is not that people are bad. But I am unable to explain. Mother-in-law's grip on the household is very tight. My mother-in-law meticulously plans every aspect of our lives, from the meals we eat to the way we spend our weekends. I am a new member of the family and am feeling too sidelined as her authority is diminishing my comfort zone. She has unwavering control over Raghu and now me too.

Despite my best efforts to please my mother-in-law, though pleasing others is not my basic nature, I find myself blamed for the smallest of mishaps. If a dish wasn't prepared to her exacting standards or if the house wasn't impeccably clean, I have to bear the brunt of her frustrations. Yet, I am trying to be patient. She just does not understand the struggles that I am facing in adjusting to my new role in the family. One evening, as the family gathered for dinner, tensions reached a boiling point. I had meticulously planned a lavish meal for Raghu's colleagues, but a power disrupted from her as it did not meet her standards and her fixed menu. Frustrated and embarrassed, she lashed out at me, blaming me for every silly thing.

At that moment, I stood my ground. I gently reminded her of the importance of compassion and understanding in family relationships. My mother-in-law made a huge hue and cry of it and started to Bangalore to your place. I am feeling like crying, Avani. I was so emotionally secure and comfortable at my Father's home. I was a bubbly and happy girl who was so happy there". As she spoke, she choked and broke down over the phone. Avani's heart went out to Radhika. She consoled her and spoke about the insights given by Dr.Vasantha. Avani could explain that Saroja never had bad intentions but her ways were hard to take as she genuinely had a problem. Listening to this, Radhika also felt a little composed. Avani said "Radhika, moving from father's house to husband's house is a huge transition for any woman. It requires a lot of resilience and courage. Maybe that is the reason women are chosen to move their place and not men. Unfortunately, adults do not understand how to vacate the stage for the young couple once their children get married and take over the side stage, just to guide them and not to intrude. It demands a great level of understanding and maturity. Some Women in the process of expressing themselves and putting their point across, lose grace and start taking control of others and situations instead of controlling their emotions. This is the perfect recipe for intensification of OCD symptoms. I understand it is difficult for you. But be wise Radhika. Respond instead of reacting. Don't give in yourself to this. She has a problem that needs to be addressed, period. It is not about you or her opinion about you at all. It is a conflict that prevails in herself." Radhika was impressed by Avani's wisdom and grace and paused to reflect on her actions. She realized that it was her mother in laws desire for control that blinded her to the beauty of the family she had married into and that was because of her OCD condition. With tears in her eyes, she thanked Avani as that conversation was an eye-opener. Radhika decided to be more alert and help her mother-in-law to overcome the issue and she discussed this with Raghu. Radhika and Raghu called up Saroja and told her that they were also coming down to Bangalore to the Iyengar mansion to spend time with the family. Saroja's complex disappeared and her happiness knew no bounds. She was struggling with her OCD issue as well as guilt as she felt he had hurt Radhika with her compulsive behaviour. But she was helpless.

Many families indeed face challenges when a woman in the household struggles with undiagnosed OCD. Often, the symptoms of OCD can be mistaken for personality quirks or simply brushed off as being overly particular. This lack of understanding can lead to significant stress within the family dynamic. The woman may feel isolated and overwhelmed by her intrusive thoughts and compulsive behaviours, yet unable to express her struggles due to fear of judgment or misunderstanding. Family members may become frustrated or confused by her behaviours, leading to tension and conflict within the household. Tasks may take longer to complete due to the need for everything to be done in a specific way, and the family may feel restricted by the rigid routines imposed by the woman's OCD. Without proper recognition and support, the woman's OCD can have a profound impact on family relationships, causing distress and hindering daily functioning. Families need to educate themselves about OCD and seek professional help if they suspect that a loved one is struggling with the disorder. With proper diagnosis and treatment, individuals with OCD can learn to manage their symptoms effectively, leading to improved family dynamics and overall well-being.

That weekend newly-wed couple arrived at Iyengar mansion and it was a feast of happy relationships. Raghu and Radhika took back Saroja to Chennai. After bidding them bye, Srini expressed his happiness in Avani helping Radhika. Avani told Srini, "Excellence is simply doing what you can, with what you have, where you are, as you are. It is just not doing the best , it is consistently doing your best. It is a virtue. Excellence is a virtue while Perfection is a disease!

9
No Problem at All, "WE" Will Do It!

"We often take for granted the very people who most deserve our gratitude."

– Unknown

"No problem at all, we will do it". The statement seems familiar, doesn't it? We often hear this from elders at home when someone seeks help or a favour. But most of the time, they aren't the ones assisting directly. They rely on secondary sources like children, grandchildren, daughters-in-law, friends, or other loved ones. Yes, life is about give and take, but it's crucial to contemplate how much one can stretch and accommodate others.

People who habitually take others for granted and make commitments on their behalf often display a lack of respect and empathy. They may overlook the efforts and contributions of those around them, assuming assistance will always be available without considering its impact. They not only delegate work but also provide unsolicited advice on how to do it with the right attitude. Such behaviour strains relationships, will undermine trust, and creates resentment. Individuals must recognize and appreciate the efforts of those who support them, rather than presuming on their goodwill without acknowledgement or reciprocity. Healthy and productive collaborations thrive on mutual respect and consideration. Yet, these situations occur daily, both at home and in the workplace. Often overlooked, they subtly poison our attitudes if left unanalyzed.

At Iyengar Mansion, Parthasarathy Iyengar was reading the daily newspaper on his reclining easy chair. As usual, around 11 am, Vedavalli got him his second dose of filter coffee. Just at that moment, the calling bell buzzed. Avani who was about to go to her research centre for a discussion of a project, opened the door and could see Mr. Iyengar's younger brother Chakrapani Iyengar standing with a tense face. Avani greeted and invited him. "Please come inside, uncle". Mr. Iyengar was also surprised to see his brother dropping in without prior intimation. He asked "Pani, what is the matter?" Pani replied "Pankajamma is admitted to the Jubilee Hospital next street. She had a fall yesterday night and the neighbors had called me. So I rushed, took her to the hospital and have admitted her there. She has injured her knees and ligament. So, she needs to stay in hospital for a week. Later she will be discharged it seems. Tonight I am leaving for a south India pilgrimage. Don't know what to do?" There was an air of silence and immediately Vedavalli stated "Don't worry. We will take care. We must take care of elders. She is not having her son also around. We can't just desert her." Immediately Pani took out the medicine list handed it over to Parthasarathy and asked if home food could be provided to the patient. Immediately Parthasarathy replied out of pride "This home has served the needy since decades. It is not even a question to be asked. Hot and healthy home-cooked food will be served to Pankajamma. You need not worry about that."

Pankajamma was Mr Iyengar's maternal aunt who was staying all by herself. She had lost her husband a decade ago and her son and his family were permanent residents of America. Pankajamma's pockets were loaded with currency but her life was devoid of people's support. Chakrapani and Parthasarathy would occasionally visit her and take care of her health and some needs. Despite them telling her son Ramanan about appointing a caretaker, it was never heeded as Pankajamma was a demanding and tough lady to handle.

She was a retired official from the post office and was a taxpayer for her pension. Livelihood was luxurious. She was a very straightforward person. Her statements used to be like bitter truths, unpolished and raw. It was difficult for people around to deal with her as they would feel disregarded because of her tone of speech. She was a woman of few words and very picky. Her conversations were ultra short and to the point like ATM transactions! Now a great project was awaiting Iyengars to take care of Pankajamma. Though it was the Iyengar couple, the actual person who was about to get into this acid test was Avani!

Avani's empathy and her inability to say NO to others. Whether it was volunteering for community events, babysitting for her neighbours, or taking on extra tasks at work, Avani always said yes, eager to lend a hand wherever she could. This quality in her was her biggest weakness as well as strength. She was a person of values and always believed in being of help to others. But sometimes, at the cost of her inner peace, it burdened her a lot. Vedavalli and Parthasarathy were always proud of Avani's good quality of "Obedience" and Avani also used to keep up to their mark, never even using her discretion that sometimes it was beyond her scope of work. She used to struggle to understand that it was okay to say No.

Vedavalli said, "Avani let me make some healthy delicious soup for Pankajamma. Avani, can you please adjust your part-time work schedule accordingly for this week? Anyways, Ramanan has been informed to come down to take care of her. He said he would be coming down here only for a week with his wife. He will take care of her staying with us".

Parthasarathy added "A successful hardworking gentleman. The last time I saw him was before his wedding when he flew to America. It will be nice to have them with us." But Avani asked, "Next week will be the children's exam schedule and having so many guests, attending a patient will be extremely difficult." Parthasarathy said, "till my wife and myself are there, no one needs to worry. We are here to take care. Why you should worry? You people take care of your schedules. Earlier days, we never used to bother about the inflow of guests. That was our rich culture! The younger generation these days is very inefficient. For making small adjustments and arrangements, they get worked up!" Avani was furious to listen to this. Every time, this used to be the scenario. Mr. and Mrs. Iyengars' entitled pride never was in sync with their actions. They used to get committed to serving others magnanimously and they outsourced the work comfortably to Avani and later took pride in having obedient sons and daughters-in-law.

Sreeja, the elder daughter-in-law came back from the office in the evening and came to know about the upcoming week's scene. She said "I am leaving the kids at my mother's place as I have to travel onsite for Germany for a week. So, you people please do not count on me for any help." She was amazingly clear on things that she never wanted to do and was lucky enough to get situations accordingly which would sync with the reasons. Avani used to strive a lot to speak. Her clear ideas could comfortably travel to the throat. But always used to get stuck there, later those suppressed words would start becoming a huge tree in her mind triggering a lot of controversial self-talk. Though she could exhibit perfect harmony outside, she used to fail to bring that harmony inside. There was a strong rift between her two selves-the rational self and her ideal self!

Avani called and informed her boss at the office to reschedule the project meeting for the coming week as there was some medical emergency at home. She took the soup and left for the hospital. She slowly opened the door and entered the ward where Pankajamma was sleeping on her bed. She smiled at her and Pankajamma stared at Avani for a while. With a serious countenance. Avani came near Pankajamma and asked " How are you, Aunty?" Pankajamma replied " Where is your mother-in-law Vedavalli? She has appointed you now for my care, is it? Why should you come? I have my great son who is sitting in America. I think he and his wife would have informed him to come right? Why you people should leave all your duties and take care of me? I can't enter into this obligatory mode in life" Avani felt a little shaky seeing the anger of Pankajanmma. Pankajamma said "I like to be independent and don't want to depend on anyone". Avani poured the hot soup into a bowl and offered it to Pankajamma on her hospital bedside table. While Pankajamma took the soup bowl, Avani looked into her eyes and said "All we human beings are interdependent and the concept of independence is obscure." Pankajamma said "You are very different Avani. I always see you as an intelligent foolish girl" and gave a smile. Avani smiled back. Pankajamma continued" You are in your in-laws' house, that too in this generation where women fight for liberation and independence. At this age, I get annoyed when your mother-in-law Vedavalli acts as a dominating instruction manual. I don't understand, being educated, being such a wise girl, why are you not on your own?" Avani did not have an answer for this. Since childhood, she never knew the concept of "staying on your own"! She was very expansive with people around her and knew only that way of life.

From dawn till dusk, Avani's days were filled with caring for her husband, children, and elderly parents and in-laws. Her life revolved around the needs of her family, and she took immense pride in fulfilling her roles as a wife, mother, daughter and daughter-in-law. She had never known the concept of independence or freedom beyond the boundaries of her familial duties. She had the small world of her research, friends, family, and a circle of relatives, where she found joy and fulfilment in nurturing her loved ones and upholding the traditions passed down through generations. Her days were spent reading, listening to music, gardening, a few research discussions in her part-time office, tending to the household chores, preparing delicious meals with recipes inherited from her grandmother, and ensuring that every member of the family was taken care of with love and devotion. She found solace in the familiar rhythm of her daily routine, finding meaning and purpose in her role as the heart of her family. Avani's happiness lay in the simple pleasures of spending time with her loved ones and sharing laughter and stories. For her, the bonds of family were sacred, and she found fulfilment in nurturing those bonds with unwavering devotion. Though she may have never known the concept of independence in the way the world outside her understood it, her heart was full, knowing that she was surrounded by the love and warmth of her family, her most precious treasure of all. Her interaction with Pankajamma held a different lens to her view of life. For the first time, Avani started looking into her beliefs. Pankajamma's confident tone triggered a lot of questions in Avani's mind.

Pankajamma asked "Tell me, Avani, it is no doubt very thoughtful of you to go outside your capacity and help me. But dear, I am not on your primary duty list. When your in-laws directed you to serve me, what made you accept just without questioning? Don't you have so many things on your plate to handle? I know Partha. Your great father-in-law. He is committed to helping others. But he will not turn up. He will order others to do the work. I am a very principled lady. I know I sound very rude. But why should you do it? I don't want to trouble you." Avani felt what Pankajamma was saying was right.

Pankajamma said "Out of my experience I am telling you Avani, blind obedience is a curse. It blinds your intellect. To avoid falling into the trap of manipulation in the name of obedience, one needs to cultivate critical thinking skills, assertiveness, and healthy boundaries. They should question requests that don't align with their values or best interests, seek support from trusted friends or advisors, and be wary of individuals who seek to exploit their obedience for personal gain. Please relook into your actions. Most of the time, when others' urgency is being imposed on you as your duty and if you are forced to accept, you are acting out of fear not out of love or obedience!" This statement was a different perspective when compared to Avani's and a thought-provoking trigger for Avani!

Everyone was scared of Pankajamma's sharp tongue. But Avani found her extremely affectionate and magnetic. She felt she had lots to learn from Pankajamma and she decided she would keep coming over to the hospital the following week to take care of her. She started looking forward to such conversations. Even Pankajamma felt very comfortable with Avani's pure intentions and she felt warmth in her company. She started looking forward to Avani's pleasant talks, her tasty simple and nutritious food that she used to bring, mindfully cooked for her health conditions. Pankajamma melted in Avani's care.

It was Friday morning. Avani got breakfast to Pankajamma and was told that she was going to get discharged that afternoon. She said " Aunty, we will go home. I have set the room for you and till you get healed, you can stay there comfortably". Pankajamma was going through a magazine lying on her bed. She removed her spectacle and made a sarcastic comment "Wow nice! you have made all arrangements and my son and daughter-in-law will come like chief guests to your house is it?" Avani tried to explain "Aunty why are you so bitter about them? Your son and daughter-in-law are professionals who work in abroad companies. Even their life is not easy. They have chosen that path. You are not ready to go and stay there as you want to have your independence. When they come, they need a place to stay, right? You have been here for the last week, so my in-laws planned that anyway, ours is a functional kitchen and all of you can be accommodated there till you resume back to your regular health. Calm down. Do not lose your temper"

Pankajamma was taken aback by Avani's naïve thinking. She said " Avani, I can't believe that you belong to this era! Since you are very straight, the world appears straight to you. Let me explain. I am in no way saying that my son or daughter-in-law should not stay abroad. I am more than happy when they are independent. But everything starts with intention Avani. Intentions must be pure and flawless. He is there abroad because if they get stuck here, I am an obligation to them. That is what they feel. Our ways are different and certainly, I cannot stay with them under one roof. But when they come, they cannot behave like guests. They came to know I was in hospital. As his duty, He should have called Parthasarathy and enquired and made arrangements over the phone. Why should Partha or Pani take the initiative to do everything and then inform him? My daughter-in-law is still not having time to call me up and enquire what happened. I am not seeking their sympathy. But why that disconnected feeling? One cannot afford to have any preference or prejudice when it comes to duty. We don't share good chemistry is a different thing and they need to do their duties when parents are sick are two different aspects in two different compartments. They must have that discretion. My daughter-in-law could have spoken to you or Vedavalli and when they came down, she could have taken the initiative to clean my existing home and made arrangements there so we could have stayed there. It wouldn't have troubled you right? Why we must all come to your heritage mansion and trouble all you people just because the house is spacious? These things irk me a lot.

Avani, Since my childhood, even I have been nurtured in a joint family and have tasted it's waters. Ideally, a joint family is successful when everyone has give and take attitude. All must have a sense of inclusion towards others. Otherwise, only one person will be slogging to keep the chorus intact and all others will be over-free-willed and will be playing non-cooperation. That is unfair. I can sense the pulse of selfish intentions very quickly, that has made me a stone. I was also a very emotional person like you. In a hard way, I had to learn that I need to first stand up for myself and later I must think of others.

All of you have your routines and we can't barge in with our demands on you. I am not for it. I know tomorrow they will come down. They both are comfort seekers and they don't read the room. Thoughtfulness is not even there in dictionary of those entitled people. With reason of jet lag, they will rest for two days. You all need to supply them coffee lunch snacks and dinner from time to time. They will be least bothered to even think that others are giving their time to them to make them feel comfortable. Avani, whenever they come down, just because you people provide more comfort in all ways, we can't encash it every time. I am tired of this. It stains my self-respect. When I try to order food from outside, your rigid mother-in-law who thinks she is eternally efficient, gives a lecture series on why you are not supposed to eat outside food and your father-in-law will join to make it an orchestra. By God's grace, their health is good, and they have accommodative children and daughters-in-law who will be their source of help. Vedavalli can run the show because she has all the resources and help. But I do not have that type of help. But I do not want to trouble them. So, I try to help them by ordering food so I can reduce their burden a bit at least. But they never acknowledge that. I keep hearing sarcastic comments from your in-laws that Pankajamma is one lazy woman who prefers to eat outside all the time. When intentions are disregarded, I become bitter Avani. People who blindly form opinions and judge others will not know their dark and difficult side at all. They will just not keep their opinions to themselves, even worse, they will induce and spread them in the air. I have seen this in families as well as in the workplace. In the name of helping others, they intrude. I always feel that "mind your business is the best policy" Because of this policy of mine, people have labelled me as antisocial."

"So, today I need to come to your mother-in-law's house, is it? She gave a sarcastic smile and said "Avani this is the best revenge you can take on me". Avani burst out into laughter. Afternoon, Srini wound up soon from the office and came to complete the discharge formalities at the hospital. Pankajamma again with a grin asked Srini "Where is your great father who is taking care of me? On the easy chair? Why do you need to take off from work and come only for this sake? You both husband and wife are setting the wrong expectations. This will harm you more in future than helping". Srini said, "when I was a small child, you were my storyteller aunty, you have always told me helping others is good!" And gave a sarcastic smile. Immediately Pankajamma reverted "But help using your discretion. Do use your brains and don't feed injustice". Pankajamma always liked Srini and Avani more than all the members of the Iyengar mansion.

Avani had a big lesson to learn from Pankajamma and that was about how to think rationally without bias. Sometimes Avani was blind to reason, she often found herself engulfed in a tempest of emotions, unable to navigate through life's challenges. With proper care at the hospital, Pankajamma was feeling much better. Vedavalli had made all arrangements for Pankajamma. Pankajamma said she would stay in the outhouse. It was rented to Seethamma and since Seethamma was on pilgrimage for two months, she had given her house keys to Vedavalli and told her "You and your guests, please feel free to use my room". Srini and Avani brought Pankajamma home. She was limping and slowly sat down on a chair. She told Vedavalli, "Vedavalli, I prefer to stay in the outhouse." Vedavalli said, "I can't monitor you if you stay in out-house! I have arranged the downstairs room for you. Pankajamma said, "as it is you all are taking trouble. Let me rest in out-house". Vedavalli said "As you wish. Avani will help you out if you need something". Pankajamma got furious. "Why are you telling this on behalf of Avani? If she can, let her offer!" Vedavalli swallowed her anger in the throat. Though she was burning inside, she knew she could never win an argument with Pankajamma. Vedavalli informed her that the next day her son and daughter -in -law will be coming down. Immediately Pankajamma said "Please tell them to take care of me. They are not here on a holiday to enjoy the Indian eateries and visit places. Since you have informed them that I am injured, they are coming to see me."

The next day, Pankajamma and Avani were discussing the story of Mahabharata over their cup of coffee. Her son Ramanan and his wife Sujatha landed in the cab. They were greeted and welcomed by all at Iyengar mansion and they went to see Pankajamma. Ramanan started his lecture " Amma, how are you? I tell you a hundred times that you need to be careful. See now there is ligament and joint damage!" Pankajamma sarcastically replied "What do my son, my life is very boring. So, I wanted some attention. I chose to fall and break my ligament!" Ramanan got furious "You haven't changed a bit. When I talk out of concern, look the way you reciprocate!" Pankajamma said " What type of concern is that when you did not arrive when I got into the hospital but you came down for the weekend followed by a long holiday?!" Ramanan bent his head. Pankajamma said "anyways you people are here, we will go back home. Let us not trouble Partha and their family". Immediately Sujatha replied " Actually we had some more work tied up with this visit. We have some bank jobs, and investment plans and also need to visit a few friends. So will be difficult if we shift home. Can't manage the kitchen along with these schedules." Pankajamma became a thunderstorm. She shouted " Then why did you come in the excuse of taking care of me? Why people here should take care of me when I am down? Don't they have their routines? I am not expecting anything from you. But you are exploiting others without taking care of your duties and I am not Okay with that. You people, like guests, keep attending to your work and Avani, under her in-law's guided instructions will take care of me. What justice is that?" Pankajamma said that Ramanan and Sujatha must feel ashamed of themselves for neglecting their mother and not doing their duties. She observed their selfish behaviour, their disregard for her comfort, and catering only for their own constant demands. Instead of succumbing to their wishes, Pankajamma decided to teach them a valuable lesson.

The next day, Sujatha and Ramanan got ready to go to a nearby restaurant to have breakfast. Vedavalli insisted that they should have breakfast at home. She said "Ramanan, I have made special masala dosa. You like the dosa that I make right?" Pankajamma blurted out "Vedavalli, at this age, you need a certificate from youngsters for your dosa? Will you keep making dosas for them?" Vedavalli grinned " No Avani is making it ready for them".Pankajamma's fury knew no bounds. "Avani, come here. You said you need to work on that project right? Are you working with dosa and pan for the project? Please drop this and go. All these people are adults. Ramanan is not a guest at this house. If they feel like eating dosas, they will make it for themselves. You please get back to your work." Avani was amazed to see Pankajamma's courage and unbiased justful thinking. She was taken aback by her clarity. Avani was inspired to see that Pankajamma's thoughts, words and actions were in perfect alignment. She sounded like a realized soul! Avani gave a thankful smile at Pankajamma, got ready to office, took her laptop and drove to her office.

Pankajamma called Ramanan and Sujatha to sit near her and spoke with such wisdom and clarity that Ramanan and Sujatha were left speechless. Pankajamma recounted tales of her struggles, her sacrifices, and her unwavering love for her family. She showed them a mirror to their selfish attitude, making them realize the error of their ways.

Pankajamma's practical wisdom began to resonate with Avani too. She started questioning her blind obedience and started asserting herself more confidently. With Pankajamma's guidance, Avani discovered her strength and voice. Over time, Avani slowly transformed into a confident and independent woman, no longer bound by the shackles of blind obedience. Pankajamma smiled with pride, knowing that she had played a small part in opening the eyes of a young lady to the power of practical thinking and self-reliance.

10

When the Wrong Roles Rule

"When you allow the people to play wrong roles and to have power over your life, you end up with the wrong results."

– Unknown

In the closely knit family of the Iyengar mansion, (rather too closely knit), sometimes, in the process of helicopter parenting of Parthasarathy and Vedavalli, sons and daughters-in-law used to get depleted of breathing space which the Iyengar couple failed to understand. Since Avani was spending more time with them than others at home, her sensitive nerves always used to get choked with this feeling. Avani's primary duties also used to be taken over by them in the name of concern and care. Avani always used to feel that she was working for a Business Process Outsourcing unit and was never for her own company! As a homemaker, her nesting and nurturing instincts were overflowing. But unfortunately, it was never given centre stage as Vedavalli was the heroine of the house in the second innings also. Despite the entire world applauding the family's close-knit bonding. That inner voice of strong rebellion from inside Avani was getting suppressed badly by Avani's gentle denial.

Her days unfolded in a delicate dance of obligations and responsibilities, primarily dictated by her dominating in-laws. From the moment she entered the family as a young bride, Avani felt the weight of expectations pressing down upon her slender shoulders. Her every move scrutinized, her every decision second-guessed, she found herself suffocating beneath the weight of tradition and duty. The Iyengar couple, with their rigid beliefs and unbending rules, ruled over the household with an iron fist. Avani was expected to conform, to suppress her desires and dreams in service to the family. Her voice became a whisper, her ambitions faded into the background as she navigated the framework of familial expectations. This happened because she was very naïve and was not alert enough to stand up for herself. It was not a huge battle to win that was in front of her. But, there were small grains of sand in her shoe that were making her journey painful. Some problems, only a wearer knows where the shoe pinches. Can never be explained to others.

Especially in an Indian household, when a girl gets married, a husband will be her solace. But especially in a joint family, the way things take a rigid shape, the husband sometimes becomes powerless to shield his wife from the suffocating embrace of his family's dominating rules. He also will be suffering as he will also be ensnared in the web of so-called "tradition", unable or unwilling to challenge the status quo. Avani's situation was no different. Avani found herself adrift, drowning in a sea of obligations with no shore in sight. Each day blurred into the next, a monotonous cycle of chores and obligations. Her dreams, once vivid and vibrant, now lay dormant, buried beneath layers of conformity. She longed to break free, to spread her wings and soar above the constraints that bound her. But the weight of the rigid routines in the name of "tradition" held her firmly in place, a prisoner of her own making. As a result, Avani remained trapped, a silent witness to her suffocation. Her spirit wilted beneath the oppressive gaze of her in-laws, her dreams fading like shadows in the harsh light of reality. A solution to this situation in the form of reflective learning was waiting for her right around the corner!

It was exactly the opposite scenario in next door Vimala's house. Vimala and Vedavalli were neighbours for more than four decades. Vimala was extremely flexible, yet strong like grass, unlike Vedavalli. She had lost her husband just around the time when her son Rajesh got married to Anvitha. Vimala was a very dynamic and enterprising woman who had a lot of clarity about her life. She was a person of few words and was a friend of herself. She was spiritually inclined and more detached from worldly life. But she used to enjoy different facets of life without any dogmas and hooks. Vedavalli had a strong opinion about Vimala that she was not so "home-oriented" type. Vimala's daughter-in-law Anvita was a very home-oriented person who believed in meticulous and elaborate protocols. She believed in hard work but could never work smart like her mother-in-law. She was a working woman who was obsessive about household chores and struggled to balance both. Even here, like in the Iyengar mansion, mother-in-law and daughter-in-law were chalk and cheese.

Grass on the other side is always greener. But we fail to water ours. Whenever Anvita used to meet Vedavalli, she used to feel that she was intensely caring, concerned and inclusive, unlike her mother-in-law Vimala. Whenever Avani used to see Vimala she always used to admire her for the sensible boundaries she used to maintain with people, unlike Vedavalli. ***The mind's cravings are like shadows, alwaysreaching for what is beyond grasp!***

It was a Friday morning and Anvita and Vimala dropped into Iyengar's mansion. Anvita had to take Avani's library book. Avani's little son was not keeping well. Avani had been to her research centre for some time for her work and Vedavalli and Parthasarathy were stuck to the child. Anvita was impressed to see the Iyengar couple's love for the grandchild and said "Aunty your grandchildren are super lucky to get care like this" and she gave a sarcastic comparison look towards Vimala. Vimala was mature enough to ignore it with a smile. Vimala asked Vedavalli "Veda why what happened? " Vedavalli started "Yesterday Avani took him for an ice cream. I kept on telling her not to do that. I know my grandchildren's tendency. They catch a cold". Vimala reverted "Veda, it is a mild fever, hydrate him well, give him paracetamol, let him rest and he will be okay. Why are you exaggerating this? By the way, parents will know what works for their kids ". Vedavalli continued "I just lose my mood if my grandchildren fall sick. These modern-day mothers just do not know how to give the right care for children". Vimala got irked with this statement " Veda, Avani takes care of all at home so well. Why are you passing this statement?" Vimala pulled Avani's little son and made him sit on her lap and started engaging him with stories and riddles. Meanwhile Vedavalli as usual prepared nice strong filter coffee for all of them. Avani's little one became much more active and ran to play. Vimala took the coffee and said "See Veda how he cheered up like a deer! Stop giving energy to problems!"

The next day Vimala went to her terrace to have a morning walk. she saw Vedavalli on her next terrace sobbing. Vimala called out "Veda what happened? After seeing Vimala, Vedavalli could not hold her tears back, she started sobbing all the more. Vimala rushed down her terrace and went to the next Iyengar mansion terrace to talk to Vedavalli.

Vimala asked " Veda, what happened? Why are you crying, that too early in the morning? All well?" Vedavalli said "Except for me all is well" Vimala got a sigh of relief and proceeded to console her. This was not a new scene between these two neighbours. Vedavalli was a person who was obsessively meticulous at work and she failed to draw boundaries. For her, it was her magnanimous inclusive nature towards others. She could hardly understand that it was more intrusive than inclusive for others. Boundaries meant "selfish" for her. She failed to manage her emotions.

Vedavalli's daughters-in-law, Sreeja and Avani, were quite different from each other. Sreeja was a modern woman, balancing a career with motherhood, while Avani, though she was a working woman, was more traditional, cherishing the age-old customs and rituals. Despite their differences, both daughters-in-law loved their children dearly and often sought Vedavalli's guidance in parenting.

One day, Vedavalli noticed Sreeja struggling to manage her work commitments along with the demands of her energetic twins, Rohan and Rahul. Sensing an opportunity to help, Vedavalli began offering unsolicited advice. "Sreeja, when I raised your husband, I used to make him drink this herbal concoction every morning. It made him strong and focused. You should try it with the twins," Vedavalli would say, handing Sreeja a jar filled with a pungent mixture of herbs. Sreeja, trying to be polite, would nod and thank her mother-in-law, but secretly wondered if the concoction would benefit her modern-day children.

On another occasion, Avani was preparing a traditional dish for her family when Vedavalli intervened. "Ah, Avani! That's not how we make it in our house. Let me show you the right way," Vedavalli insisted, taking over the kitchen and demonstrating her culinary skills. Avani, although appreciative of her mother-in-law's expertise, felt a pang of insecurity. She wondered if she was living up to Vedavalli's expectations as the keeper of traditions. Vedavalli 's well-intentioned advice, because they were given even in unnecessary situations, began to feel more like interference to Sreeja and Avani. They started to feel overwhelmed and frustrated, longing for some space and autonomy in parenting. That morning when all three women met in the kitchen for coffee, Sreeja and Avani decided to have a heart-to-heart with Vedavalli.

"Amma, we appreciate all that you do for us and the children. Your love and wisdom are invaluable to us. But sometimes, we need to find our way as mothers," Sreeja started hesitantly. Avani nodded in agreement, "We want our children to grow up with the values and traditions that you hold dear, but we also want to incorporate our own beliefs and methods of parenting. Please allow us to go through this journey. Stop mothering the second innings!"

Vedavalli, taken aback by their frank opinion, paused and then said, "My dear daughters-in-law, I only want what's best for the children. You people are making allegations instead of thanking me? Tears started filling her eyes. Vedavalli's tears ignited Parthasarathy's impulsive anger and he started talking in a high pitch " Why are you concerned about them? They do not need us anymore. Please understand. In our last few days of our lives do you need all this blame?". Always it was very disappointing to the sons and daughters-in-law that they could never put their point across in a way the Iyengar couple could understand. Their ego was so big that hardly others' opinions of feelings were heard! This was the reason for Vedavalli shedding tears. She narrated the instances as a complaint to Vimala.

"Vedavalli," Vimala began softly, "I've noticed the deep love you have for your children. But I also sense a certain attachment that brings you worry and distress". Vedavalli looked up, surprised by Vimala's words. "What do you mean Vimala? Isn't it natural for a mother to worry about her children? Do you know how much I love my children and grandchildren?" Vimala nodded, "It is natural to love and care for your children, but it is important to understand the difference between love and attachment. Love is selfless, and unconditional, and brings joy and happiness. Love always puts the other person's happiness as first priority. Attachment, on the other hand, is possessive, filled with expectations, and can lead to worry and suffering. It puts only the likes and dislikes of oneself first as priority"

Vedavalli frowned, trying to grasp Vimala's words. "But how do I differentiate between the two? I love my children dearly and want the best for them". Vimala sat down beside Vedavalli and explained, "Love allows your children to grow and flourish, respecting their choices and giving them the freedom to live their own lives. Attachment, however, binds them to you, creating expectations and conditions that can stifle their growth and happiness."

Vedavalli listened intently, realizing the truth in Vimala's words. She thought about the times she had interfered in her daughters-in-law's lives, driven by her worries and attachment. Vimala continued, "It is important to strike a balance between love and detachment. Love them unconditionally, support them in their endeavours, but also give them the space and freedom to make their own choices, even if they differ from yours." Vedavalli nodded slowly, "I understand, Vimala. I have been so caught up in my worries and attachment that I failed to see the harm it was causing. I will strive to love my children with detachment, respecting their individuality and choices."

Vimala smiled, "That's the spirit, Veda. Remember, true love is free from fear and attachment. It is a source of strength and joy, bringing happiness to both the giver and the receiver". For a change, Vedavalli looked receptive without defending herself. Vimala, seeing Vedavalli's receptive state, decided to delve deeper into the wisdom of the scriptures to further enlighten her about the concept of Ashrama Dharma."Vedavalli," Vimala began, "Our ancient scriptures beautifully define the stages of life or 'Ashrama Dharma' that guide us on the path of harmonious living. These stages are designed to help individuals fulfil their duties and responsibilities at different phases of life in the right way."

She continued, "The four Ashramas are: Brahmacharya (student life), Grihastha (householder life), Vanaprastha (retired life), and Sannyasa (renunciate life). Each stage has its own set of duties and responsibilities, preparing us for the next stage and ultimately leading us towards spiritual growth and liberation."

Vedavalli listened intently, intrigued by the wisdom of the ancient scriptures.Vimala explained further, "In the Grihastha Ashrama, which is the stage of household life where most of us find ourselves, the scriptures emphasize the importance of fulfilling one's duties towards family, society, and ancestors. It teaches us to live a life of righteousness, love, and compassion, balancing our responsibilities and relationships with detachment." She added, "The Grihastha stage teaches us to love our family members unconditionally, support them in their endeavours, and contribute to the welfare of society. But it also reminds us to let go of attachment and expectations, understanding that each individual has their path and destiny." The roles are so well defined and after grihastashrama, once we enter Vanaprastha, our roles are unfit to rule and navigate the family boat!

Vedavalli nodded, beginning to see the relevance of Ashrama Dharma in her own life. "So, Vimala, what you're saying is that by understanding and embracing the principles of Ashrama Dharma, we can live a life of harmony, balance, and spiritual growth?" Vimala smiled warmly, "Exactly, Veda. Ashrama Dharma provides us with a framework for leading a meaningful and fulfilling life. It teaches us to perform our duties selflessly, love unconditionally, and cultivate detachment, thereby fostering harmonious relationships and inner peace. **However, when wrong roles dominate our lives, it can lead to imbalance, discontent, and disharmony within ourselves and our communities**. "

Vedavalli felt a sense of clarity and peace wash over her. She told Vimala innocently "When did you learn so much? I always see you looking only into your life and I hardly see you spend time at home!" Vimala didn't know what to say for that blunt statement of Vedavalli. She laughed loudly and told her "I love my family, Veda. But I am detached. I can't take over Anvita's role in taking care of my grandchild. No doubt I do help her. But I need to respect her boundaries and stop there. If I start dominating her and like a Hitler, I dictate parenting rules for her, her creativity as a mother gets snubbed and that results in toxic emotions. Children should be held in our palms gently like sand Veda. If you tighten the fist, the sand will slip off your palms. Don't hold it tight. It will stay. Detached parenting is not about absence, but about presence with freedom; it's loving deeply while letting go lightly". Vedavalli thanked Vimala with a smile. By the time their conversation was over, Vedavalli could hear Avani screaming "Amma, I need to send Saketh to school. I am unable to find his school sweater! Vedavalli rushed down the stairs screaming back "Wait I have changed the arrangement of clothes in his wardrobe. You will not find it. Let me come and show you!" Vimala made a frowned face and murmured to herself "Irreparable attachment chains us to expectations, blinding us to the beauty of letting go!". She walked away from Iyengar's mansion to resume back to her routine.

Bluntness may be swift, but its impact is lasting and irreparable!

11

The Journey Inward-Discovery of Self

"The privilege of a lifetime is to become who you truly are."

– Carl Jung

On a Saturday morning, Avani went to a nearby supermarket to buy the month's groceries home. She shopped everything in the cart and was waiting at the billing counter. There was some issue with the software in the billing system and the staff of the supermarket were busy setting things right. The queue was getting longer and longer and people waiting in the queue were getting restless. An old man standing in front of Avani in the queue was the only person there who was calm and composed and he did not even bother to enquire the staff as to when the queue would move. That caught Avani's attention. Avani kept on getting phone calls from home in between. Once Vedavalli called to add a few more things to her provision list. Next, Parthasarathy called to find out where his shopping bag was. This call was followed by her children to find out where their football studs were. After some time, people started staring at Avani as if she was tagged to a GPS tracker! She kept on answering every phone call on her cell phone. The next strange call was by her maid. While struggling to manage her cell phone to the ear and her heavy luggage, the call got switched to the speaker mode and there the maid Lakshmi was as loud as a politician addressing a huge gathering! "Madam, I can't wait for long. If you are not coming early, I will leave. I will clean the garage next week. I have so many houses to work for. You can't keep me waiting" The entire crowd around started staring at Avani and it was very embarrassing for her! She slowly switched off the speaker mode after the call. The old man next to Avani turned towards her and offered Avani to move ahead of him in the queue with a smile. Avani felt it was a thoughtful gesture. "That's ok sir. Thanks. I have a huge list to be billed. You hardly have three to four items. Please finish yours. I think the billing computer will get set right in some time".

That old tall man continued the conversation. "I am Dr. Krishnamurthy. Young lady, may I know your good name? Where do you stay?" "I am Dr. Avani and I stay in 17th Cross, two roads parallel to this main road." "Oh! I stay in the building on the next road to yours" Said Krishnamurthy. Avani was surprised! "Sir, we are quite old to this area and I have not seen you earlier!" He said "I recently moved last week. Did you see that corner white house? I have moved there. On the first floor". Avani replied "oh that building! I saw a big board on that building something about journaling. I don't recall". Dr. Krishnamurthy said "I conduct sessions on mindful journalling and also I have my clinic where I conduct counselling sessions". Avani asked "You said you are a doctor. What is your specialization?" "I am not a medical doctor. I have a PhD in psychology from Stanford. I consult and conduct counselling sessions. Also, I do conduct journaling sessions". Avani said, "Sounds Interesting!" Krishnamurthy said, "You said you are Dr Avani are you a practicing doctor?" "No, I am an environmental scientist". Krishnamurthy said, " good to hear." Was nice to meet you, lady. Please do drop in some time". Avani said "My pleasure sir. Will surely do". Even amidst that busy tight schedule, Dr Krishnamurthy's calm countenance and wisdom-radiating personality got captured in Avani's mind. He was a stranger but Avani felt like she wanted to talk more. The term "journalling" started lingering in her mind and she wanted to explore more. She thought that he was easily close to 80 years. But looked so active and fit brimming with energy!

Avani was thinking that she should take up some activity to rejuvenate herself. Every day, Avani would wake up before dawn to prepare breakfast for the family, perform her morning prayers, and then start her daily chores. She took care of everyone's needs, from her husband to her in-laws, from her children to her nephews. Amidst this regular hustle and bustle, she used to make time for her research, webinars and some environment-based activities at her research centre which used to be thrice or four times a month. But amidst the chaos of the joint family, Avani often felt lost, like a shadow blending into the background. She began to wonder about her own identity. Was she just a wife, a mother, a daughter-in-law? Or was there more to her? The voices of the family members seemed to drown out her desires and dreams. Their validation became her priority, and she often suppressed her feelings and aspirations to please others. One evening, as Avani sat alone in her room, she was feeling suffocated. Between what she was doing and what she wanted to do, there was a lot of disparity. She decided it was time for some introspection. She took out a diary she had hidden away, a place where she penned down her thoughts, dreams, and aspirations. As she flipped through the pages, she realized how much of herself she had buried over the years.

Fascinated by the idea of exploring her thoughts and feelings through writing, she thought of signing up for mindful journaling sessions conducted by Dr. Krishnamurthy hoping it might offer her some solace and healing. The next day evening, Avani went to Dr Krishnamurthy's house and there on the balcony, she saw him engrossed in sorting a few letters. The gentle and cosy ambience of Dr . Krishnamurthy's cabin enveloped a warmth around Avani. Dr. Krishnamurthy saw Avani and welcomed her "Hello Avani, what a pleasant surprise! Please be seated. So, what brings you here?" Avani said "I was very curious about this journalling workshop. So wanted to know about it. Krishnamurthy paused for a while and said "Well, in a nutshell, I can say, Journalling is you screaming on paper! When you have some thoughts running in your mind, any thought, positive or negative, there is no outlet for it. You will be internalizing it. But when you put it on paper, it is out! You can see your problem in words outside of you. Once you have externalized the problem, it's no more inside you!" Avani exclaimed "Interesting! Will it work?" "Of course, try it yourself!" Said Krishnamurthy. Krishnamurthy who was a compassionate and skilled journalling expert introduced Avani to the therapeutic power of journaling. He emphasized the importance of self-reflection, mindfulness, and self-expression as tools for emotional healing and personal growth.

Avani asked, "So when can we start?" "The best time is now. Young lady, pick up the pen and paper there, here is your seat, you can start" Avani was taken aback! She just picked up the pen and paper and asked him." What should I write? Krishnamurthy looked deep into her eyes and said "are you happy with whatever you are doing in your life?" Avani gave a confused look. Immediately Krishnamurthy reframed his words "Ok, let us keep it simpler. Are you happy with the activities you are doing from morning till night in all the portfolios you take up, maybe at home or the office or any workplace of yours?" There is a popular message in our scriptures, *When the student is ready, the teacher arrives!* Avani was ready for her introspection and there the teacher in the form of Krishnamurthy was to help!

Krishnamurthy said "No one is going to read or evaluate your writing here. Be honest and true to yourself. It is like the way you open up a problem to the doctor without missing any information. You will not be judged and apart from yourself and your paper, no one else is going to hear you! take your time. I am having someone in the next cabin. They had taken an appointment for counselling. I will take an hour maybe. So please go ahead with your journalling Avani! Happy your time"! Avani was delighted! She just had a look around that cosy cabin, that silence that was all pervasive in that cabin. She just took her scribble pad and pen and started! Initially, there was editing of words that pitched in. As and when she progressed found herself opening up to her emotions in ways she had never imagined! She began to explore her fears, frustrations, and long-held beliefs that had been weighing her down for years. She went unplugged! After an hour or so, Krishnamurthy came back to Avani and asked "Still writing?" Avani said, "just finished!" He asked, "So how was the experienced lady?" Avani smiled and said," After a long time I felt I sat with myself! I thoroughly enjoyed it! So, when can I start the formal classes, sir? Let me know". Krishnamurthy smiled and said " This is a highly informal exercise. This one hour of journalling was your first step. No sessions or anything. I enjoy talking to people. players can't view their game. I am in the audience. If anyone wants my view of their game, I will just give them input. That is all.

Of course, I can help you to journal your thoughts from different perspectives if you are interested." Avani was extremely happy to come across Dr.Krishnamurthy. He was truly a healer! He said, "If you need to repair any gadget, you go to its service centre, right? If your mind is giving up, you can come to this service centre! Mixers, TVs, and mobiles are all physical gadgets. But your mind is not a physical gadget. It is made of components called thoughts. So, when thoughts intertwine and short circuit the brain, it needs servicing". Avani was extremely convinced by the analogy!

Evenings, when Avani used to send her children for their sports and art classes, she used to rush to her journalling sessions. She started enjoying it. Writing used to pump up her spirits and she used to rediscover her positive self. Each session of the workshop became a safe and nurturing space for Avani to confront her inner demons, process her emotions, and gain a deeper understanding of herself. The act of putting pen to paper allowed her to articulate her thoughts and feelings, giving her a sense of clarity and relief. With Dr.Krishnamurthy's guidance, Avani learnt to practice mindfulness in her daily life, becoming more present and aware of her thoughts, feelings, and actions. She also discovered the importance of self-care and started carving out time for herself amidst her busy schedule, whether it was through journaling, meditation, or simply taking a leisurely walk in the garden.

As the weeks turned into months, Avani began to notice a significant shift in her mindset. The constant chatter of her mind started to quieten, replaced by a sense of calm and inner peace. The emotional wounds that had once seemed insurmountable began to heal, and Avani found herself embracing life with renewed vigour and enthusiasm.

One evening, as she sat down to journal, Avani realized how far she had come since attending the workshop. She felt grateful for the transformative journey she had embarked upon and knew that she had finally found a way to heal her mind and nurture her soul. As and when her journalling session progressed Avani learnt a lot about human psychology and also, and she got a glimpse of spiritual lessons from scholarly Krishnamurthy. Discussions used to go on for hours and Avani enjoyed every bit of it.

One Sunday Avani went to Dr. Krishnamurthy for a journalling session. He was pruning the rose plants in his garden. He greeted Avani "Yes my young friend, nice to see you here. paper and pen are dragging you out quite often these days from household chores. Nice to see! Avani, just wanted to know what aspects of journalling are you enjoying.? Are you sounding like a heroine? Or are you able to see your grey and dark sides as well? This is the core of journalling Avani. Transformation cannot happen without introspection. Without introspection, it is just nourishing one's ego. Sometimes there will be a huge disparity between what we are and what we think we are! That needs to be addressed first to integrate ourselves".

Avani was taken aback. The reason she went there on a Sunday, specifically was to share her previous night's journalling experience with Krishnamurthy. "Did you read my mind? I was feeling so bad after journalling yesterday! I could see the total dark and grey shades of my personality.

I felt I couldn't recognize myself. started getting scared that was my true personality!"

Krishnamurthy gave a smile, kept aside all his garden tools, washed his hands under a garden tap, and called Avani for tea. They sat in his garden and he said "Just like the earth needs all seasons for its overall well-being, the mind needs all shades of thoughts to learn and transform. It is as simple as that. While you are seeing a "not so good face" of yours, it is ok. Accept and it will pass. Don't reside there and give reality to it. Learn to observe your mind from a distance. Then you will not take it seriously! There are so many situations when we seek validation, we deny our true feelings. Our intent may be either not to hurt others to please them or to seek their validation. Such thoughts when suppressed, turn sour, get pickled and get ejected as these grey and black thoughts. Avani, there is no need to feel bad. They are the best indicators of your failure to handle many situations not so efficiently. Just address those instead of getting agitated with external stimuli. Trust me it works amazingly. You know what, life is not about us battling with the world it's we battling with our minds! We associate strongly with our mind. That is the catch. Just see how it feels to detach from it. You are a super peaceful personality!" "Thank you, so much sir! " Avani whispered to herself, tears of gratitude streaming down her face. "You have given me the gift of self-discovery and healing. I will forever be grateful."

Avani could see changes in herself in her daily life. One day, Avani sat with her filter coffee to relish every sip of it. Vedavalli, as usual, rushed and asked her to quickly buy tomatoes from a cart vendor who was passing by in front of the Iyengar mansion. Avani calmly replied " Amma I am dead tired. Let me have coffee in peace. I will bring tomatoes later". This was a strange reaction from Avani, Vedavalli felt. Parthasarathy was furious that Srini and Avani forgot to do some bank transactions on time despite his ten reminders. Avani didn't bother to explain. It so happened one day that Vedavalli and Parthasarathy called Avani and told her that they had invited a relative's family for dinner the next evening and six of them would be coming for dinner. Avani said assertively "But tomorrow I am going to a music concert. I bought the tickets a week ago. I cannot be there." Vedavalli said " But I have told them" Avani said, " If you want me to help you in cooking amma, please change the dates and inform them." Always Avani used to be informed about things. Despite her running the show at home, she was never a decision-maker. Vedavalli could feel a blow to her ego. She had never realized that she could not take Avani's time and schedule for granted. Parthasarathy grinned "Anyways next time we should take appointments from children before committing to guests". Earlier Avani would have boarded the bus for a guilt trip with such statements. This time she gently replied" "Yes Appa. A lot of things on my plate these days. From now on let us decide it together when we call any guests home so there is no confusion and everyone's schedule is taken care of without being disturbed". Gradually, Avani realized how important it is to voice out her requirements. She was in victim mode earlier without this ability to voice out! Avani was now totally aware of where she was going wrong. She realized that other's urgency at home was being seen as her duty and that was the reason for her anxiety.

She realized that she need not be everyone's helpdesk. Not every work of the house was in her scope of work. She had never defined that frame! For her to feel happy and spread happiness around her, she had to fill her cup with happiness. She started saying "No" to unimportant things and stopped working on odds even for her closest people. She started setting boundaries and pulled back from validation mode. She became a best friend of herself. Avani prioritized self-care. She dedicated time for herself to relax, engage in activities she enjoyed, and recharge. This helped her stay calm, patient, and resilient in the face of challenges. Whenever Avani successfully started handling nagging situations assertively and constructively, she celebrated her small victories. This positive reinforcement encouraged her to continue practising assertive communication and maintain her boundaries effectively This art of mindful journalling helped her in a big way by mirroring her deeper side to her! She realized that her problem was not a nagging mother-in-law or a father who sounded over practical and transactional, but she could not deal with them confidently. It's not the load that breaks you, it's the way you carry it. Life shrinks or expands in proportion to one's courage.

As Avani continued her mindful journaling practice, she became a source of inspiration for her family, showing them the importance of prioritizing mental health and self-care. And while the challenges of joint family living persisted, Avani faced them with a newfound resilience and grace, knowing that she had the tools and inner strength to navigate life's ups and downs with ease and equanimity. She felt extremely grateful for finding a mentor like Dr. Krishnamurthy and she felt that she has so much to learn about life! Avani's journey taught her that true happiness and fulfilment come from within. By shifting her personality to positive gears and handling situations assertively, she not only improved her own life but also created a harmonious and loving environment for her entire family.

12

Liberation from Clutter, the First Step to Simplicity!

"The first step in crafting the life you want is to get rid of everything you don't want"

– Joshua Becker

Iyengar Mansion was an ancient building that bore witness to four generations of the same family. It's walls whispered stories of discipline, love, laughter, tears, and dreams. The building had seen the family grow, from the great-grandparents who first laid its foundation to the youngest members who played in its courtyards. One sunny morning, an unexpected notice arrived. Parthasarathy Iyengar was having his coffee reading a newspaper on his easy chair. Vedavalli was picking flowers from the jasmine creeper in the garden on the front side of the mansion. A team from BBMP (Bruhat Bangalore Mahanagara Palike, municipal body of Bangalore city) came with some equipment and entered the mansion. The senior engineer from that group approached Mr. Iyengar and said that BBMP is conducting a survey of all the old buildings in that area as a precautionary measure prior to the expected upcoming heavy monsoon. Mr. Iyengar raised his eyebrow sceptically and asked "how would you know the strength of my building? "This is shortly going to be a centenary building soon and it was built with excellent quality materials almost hundred years back". The engineer replied "Sir, first we will be conducting a visual inspection that can help identify signs of wear and tear, cracks, rust, or other visible defects that may indicate structural issues. Then if it is required, we will go for structural analysis which is done by a Non-destructive test (NDT)test. NDT is a computational technique used to analyze the stress, strain, and deformation of building components under various loading conditions. It helps engineers optimize the design and identify potential weak points or areas of concern." Parthasarathy, with a dual mind, gave a nod for them to go ahead. They almost conducted those tests for an hour. Finally, the senior official took a pen and paper, wrote something and signed on it. He said" Sir, this building is very old and is not fit for habitation anymore. It needs to be rebuilt or renovated with stronger materials. Our technical team will come and later perform some load testing and finally give the report. The Government will be issuing a notice shortly. The government has passed an order to demolish the buildings that are very old and fragile." The news sent shockwaves through Mr. Iyengar's nerves. He had spent his entire life within those walls. He couldn't believe his ears as that ancestral house was his pride and identity. Vedavalli overheard this and agony stuck deep down in her heart like an arrow. She entered that home as a new bride. She took off the reins of the house and it was the 50th year of her reign in continuum. She rushed from the corridor towards Mr. Iyengar who stood still after listening to the news. She turned breathless and had a fall. Immediately Parthasarathy rushed and helped her get up. He called up Avani immediately and then realized she was off to Mysore for a cousin's wedding. Avani was on speed dial list at home as she used to handle all crises responsibly. Then he dialed Srini's number and reported Vedavalli's condition. Srini immediately rushed home and took her to hospital. The doctor at the hospital immediately did an ECG and diagnosed a mild cardiac arrest. He recommended an angioplasty and recommended bed rest for Vedavalli for a month. The doctor said a stent needed to be inserted by surgery as there was a block in one of the heart valves and also expressed that her cardiac health had deteriorated. It was a bumpy ride for all at Iyengar mansion.

Vedavalli ruled the kitchen and the home with an iron fist. Her obsessive needs for control and her belief that she was indispensable in the kitchen were well-known within the family. She had always been wary of letting anyone else take charge, firmly believing that her way was the only right way. Avani was a gentle and patient woman, though lost her cool sometimes, who had always tried to navigate the delicate balance between respecting her mother-in-law's authority and asserting her capabilities. Despite her efforts, Vedavalli's dominating presence cast a long shadow over Avani's role in the household.

The confident Parthasarathy was disturbed by a series of discomforts. More with Vedavalli's health being hampered. There were a lot of changes in the Iyengar mansion. Parthasarathy's elder son Sridhar along with Sreeja and their two children moved to London as both Sridhar and Sreeja got a job there. Their children also joined a new school in London. They started their new life away from Iyengar's nest.

While the thought of children leaving the nest can be emotional and challenging for parents, it's important to remember that it's a natural part of the parenting journey. As parents, their role is to provide love, support, and guidance as children spread their wings and embark on their adventures. It's a bittersweet moment, filled with pride, excitement, and a touch of nostalgia, as parents watch children grow into independent and confident adults. But Parthasarathy and Vedavalli had a different view on this.

Usually In orthodox Indian families, especially in South India, the concept of separation from children's families can often be viewed as unconventional or even unsettling. Traditionally, the joint family system has been deeply rooted in South Indian culture, where multiple generations live together under one roof, sharing responsibilities, resources, and a strong sense of familial bonds. For many aged parents like our Iyengar couple, in this cultural context, the idea of Sridhar and Sreeja moving away and forming their separate households was perceived as a break from tradition and family unity. They were feeling a sense of loss or loneliness at the thought of being separated from their children and grandchildren, whom they had been closely connected with for years. In the joint family system, there is a shared responsibility among family members to care for the elderly, ensuring their well-being and comfort.

However, it is important to recognize that societal norms and family dynamics are evolving. As younger generations become more independent and pursue opportunities outside of their hometowns or even countries, the traditional joint family system is changing. While the concept of separation may be challenging for parents, it is essential to understand and respect the choices and aspirations of the younger generation. Open communication, understanding, and compromise can help bridge the generational gap and ease the transition toward a more independent living arrangement while still maintaining strong family ties and support networks. Well, this is at the thought level. But tough to introduce any new dimension to Iyengar's family!

Now actual load was on Avani to manage the household, kids, kitchen , taking care of Vedavalli and also ensure the comfort of Parthasarathy. The biggest of all the challenges was to vacate a load of clutter in the mansion. The things which were the treasure of Iyengar mansion but for which she could not take any ownership and dispose. This was the trickiest aspect to handle.

Vedavalli underwent angioplasty. Though the surgery was successful, her health began to decline. She had terrible mood swings as the change of house that was awaited triggered a strong discomfort in her. Her anxiety was about children decluttering her precious things! Simple tasks became challenging, and her once impeccable control over the kitchen started to waver. Despite this, she refused to acknowledge her limitations, insisting that she could manage everything on her own.

One day, as Vedavalli struggled to prepare a meal, Avani quietly stepped in to help without making a fuss. She skillfully took over the cooking, demonstrating her knowledge of traditional South Indian recipes and techniques. Instead of feeling threatened or undermined, Vedavalli watched in awe as Avani effortlessly handled the kitchen, maintaining the same standards of cleanliness and precision that she had always insisted upon.

Avani and Srini though started their life in this organized clutter, they never knew they had to take over the ownership and dispose of so many things that did not even belong to them! They met with a challenge unlike any other. The majority of that clutter, they did not own! Every corner of the mansion was filled with trunks, chests, and boxes, each holding memories and treasures from times gone by. It was as if the past had physically manifested itself, creating a maze that Avani and Srini struggled to navigate. Hundred-year-old Iyengar mansion! Its walls, adorned with fading portraits and age-old photos, whispered tales of grandeur and tradition. For Mr. and Mrs. Iyengar, each item was a piece of their history, a tangible connection to their ancestors. Letting go was not just about decluttering; it felt like parting with a piece of their soul. "These are not just things," they would say, "they are memories, traditions, our very identity."

Avani and Srini, torn between respect for their heritage and the need for space and order, embarked on a mission. They organized weekends dedicated to sorting, categorizing, and deciding what to keep, donate, or discard. It was a journey of discovery as they unearthed forgotten heirlooms, old photographs, and handwritten letters. However, with each item, came a story. A faded sari worn by a great-grandmother, a brass lamp that had lit countless ceremonies, or a cookbook with recipes passed down through generations. The emotional weight of these objects made the task both physically and emotionally draining. Slowly, but surely, progress was made. The next generation learned to compromise, preserving the essence of their heritage while making space for the present. They set up a dedicated space in the mansion to display cherished items, turning it into a mini-museum that told the story of their family. Only these items were listed to be carried forward next.

For the elders, seeing their home transformed was bittersweet. While they missed the familiarity of the clutter, they took solace in knowing that the memories were alive and honoured. It was a lesson for both generations – the importance of letting go without forgetting, of cherishing the past while embracing the future.

The biggest transformation Avani underwent was, to see how difficult it was for her in-laws to let go of their home, their hierarchy and the things which they considered as their soul! Even being so artistic and home-oriented, she felt as if she was breaking herself out from the stigma of attachments for unnecessary things. While decluttering every object, it reminded me of all the mood swings and tantrums thrown by her in-laws to take control and how they had never allowed her to move any object in the house against their wish. her past obedience sounded toxic when she recalled those moments. She threw things out mercilessly. So many people, relatives and sometimes even friends and their children who lived in that home and some who came to stay for some time for their jobs and studies, had just taken things for granted that the Iyengar mansion was store room which magnanimously would shelter all their clutter as Mr. and Mrs. Iyengar had allowed everyone around to dump their furniture or any other old stuff, because the house was very big. Also, they were the owners who could handle that. They never thought that once they age, it would be difficult for the next generation!

Vedavalli was not even ready to part with many things. Avani found it hard. She had a toxic feel towards the clutter and Mr. And Mrs. Iyengars' possessive hoardings, at the same time she had to take care of them and their well-being as they had to move to a new house where she had to take over as the lady of the house. She was torn between her dislikes and duties.

Firstly, Avani understood that her in-laws' house is filled with memories, possessions, and perhaps some emotional baggage. She needed to approach the decluttering process with sensitivity, acknowledging the importance of each item to her in-laws. Prior to the decluttering process, she took some time for self-reflection and emotional healing. She started engaging in activities that brought her joy and relaxation, such as meditation, reading, or spending time with loved ones. She spoke to her spouse and her close friends about her feelings which provided emotional support and perspective. She started establishing clear boundaries with her in-laws about the decluttering process to avoid misunderstandings and conflicts.

Avani one day came to Mr. and Mrs. Iyengars' room. Vedavalli was lying down after taking medicines and Mr. Iyengar was reading a newspaper. She discussed with them her intentions, explaining that she wanted to declutter the house to create a more organized and peaceful living environment for everyone in the new rented house that they were planning to live in, till the Iyengar mansion was rebuilt. She also explained that it was not as huge as the Iyengar mansion to house all the things that existed there. She started Involving her in-laws in the decluttering process by asking for their input and respecting their decisions about what to keep, donate, or discard. She and Srini started decluttering one room at a time, sorting items into categories (keep, donate, discard). This methodical approach made the process easier, more manageable and less overwhelming. While decluttering, she ensured to preserve important family heirlooms, photos, and mementoes. She created a designated space or memory box for these items, honouring their significance to her in-laws.

As she made progress with decluttering, she saw it as an opportunity for a fresh start. She embraced her role as the lady of the house with renewed enthusiasm and commitment. She understood that change is a natural part of life and it will help her adapt to her new responsibilities with grace and resilience.

While the house things were being shifted, Parthasarathy and Vedavalli sat on the veranda, lost in memories, gazing at the building that held their past. His grandchildren, Sanketh and Samrudh, noticed his sadness and decided to take action. They started assuring him that they would all be staying together and moving out only temporarily. They will be getting back to the same nest in a new form again! They assured him that they could face this change together and make new memories, even if in a different place. On completion of the decluttering process, they finally moved to the new rented house nearby. A new place and a new start! Avani celebrated her achievements and the positive transformation of her new home. She felt a sense of accomplishment and pride in her role as the caretaker of the household.

Throughout this journey, there was a subtle but significant shift in the household hierarchy. As she took over the responsibility of decluttering the old home and setting up the new home, she gained her in-laws' trust and respect.

They began to see her not just as a daughter-in-law but as an integral part of the family who cares deeply about their well-being and the harmony of the household. Avani won over her agitated and sad mind, pressed the refresh button on her life, and established herself as the lady of the house with love, respect, and understanding. As the days turned into weeks, Avani gradually took on more responsibilities around the house, from managing finances to organizing family events. She did so with grace and efficiency, always seeking Vedavalli's input and guidance while gently asserting her ideas and methods.

The new house was smaller than what they were used to, with modern amenities that seemed alien to the old couple. The kitchen was compact, the rooms were cosy, and the neighbourhood was bustling with activity. At first, Mr. and Mrs. Iyengar felt out of place, missing the familiarity and comfort of their old home.

Avani and Srini did their best to help the Iyengar couple settle in. They spent weekends helping them unpack boxes, arranging furniture, and setting up the new house. Despite their efforts, Mr. and Mrs. Iyengar couldn't shake off the feeling of displacement. As days turned into weeks, a subtle transformation began to take place. Avani, an avid gardener, started planting flowers in the small backyard, turning it into a vibrant oasis. Vedavalli joined her. Parthasarathy, on the other hand, took an interest in the local community, joining a group of senior citizens who met at the nearby park every morning for walks and chats. Slowly but surely, the Iyengars began to explore their new surroundings. They discovered a quaint little grocery store around the corner that stocked all their favourite ingredients. They found a nearby temple where they could continue their daily prayers. And most importantly, they met their new neighbours, who welcomed them with open arms and warm smiles.

One evening, as Mr. and Mrs. Iyengar sat on their porch sipping tea, Vedavalli looked at her husband and smiled. "You know?" she said softly, "this place is starting to feel like home." Parthasarathy nodded in agreement, taking his wife's hand in his. "It may not be our old house," he replied, "but it's our home now. And home is wherever we are together."As the months passed, the Iyengars grew more and more comfortable in their new surroundings. The rented house, once a strange and unfamiliar place, had become a sanctuary filled with love, laughter, and new memories. Avani and Srini watched with joy as they adjusted to their new life. They realized that home wasn't just a physical space but a feeling of belonging and contentment that the Iyengars had found once again. And so, the old couple, with their resilience and open hearts, showed everyone that home is not defined by walls or roofs but by the love and warmth shared within.

One evening, as they sat together in the living room of the new house, Vedavalli turned to Avani with tears in her eyes. "I never thought I would say this," she admitted softly, "but I can't manage the home anymore. I need to hand over the torch to you." Avani smiled warmly, placing a reassuring hand on Vedavalli's shoulder. "It's okay, Amma," she said gently. "We all reach a point where we need to pass on the responsibility to the next generation. I promise to take care of the home and uphold the traditions that you've taught me." When this emotional conversation was going on between mother-in-law and daughter-in-law, Srini brought up the plan of the new Iyengar mansion and showed it to Parthasarathy. Parthasarathy delved deep into the plan with an engineer's lens and appreciated and acknowledged that the new house would be a more comfortable one than their old mansion. Vedavalli added "Ensure that there are few flowering plants and jasmine creeper in the new home. That is all my requirement."

From that day on, Vedavalli began to step back and let Avani take the lead. She realized that trusting her daughter-in-law was not a sign of weakness, but rather a testament to her success in raising a capable and caring woman. As Avani took on her new role as the lady of the house, she continued to honour Vedavalli's legacy by preserving the family's traditions and values. Avani realized that **true power comes from being inclusive and expansive and not by isolating within thorny fences. Healthy boundaries and bonds are prerequisites for harmony.** Together, they formed a strong and harmonious partnership, each contributing their unique strengths to ensure the smooth functioning of the home. The torch was passed from one generation to the next, symbolizing not just a change in household responsibilities, but also a deepening of trust, respect, and love between a mother-in-law and her daughter-in-law.

www.ingramcontent.com/pod-product-compliance
Lightning Source LLC
LaVergne TN
LVHW041216150826
845673LV00001B/425

9798894159584